THE RUTHLESS BREED

The town of Coldbrook was closed tight, with ruthless old Troy Coldbrook running it, and his headstrong son, Wes, ready to destroy all comers.

And Steve Benson was his special target. He and Wes had a lot in common—they both wanted the same stretch of rangeland—and the same girl.

It was hardly a fair fight with Wes having money, power, and the lust for blood and vengeance. Benson and the other small ranchers were in trouble when all hell broke loose as holdup led to murder and murder led to range war.

Benson was being pushed hard . . . but when he was pushed he turned to iron, and iron doesn't yield.

D(wight) B(ennett) Newton is the author of a number of notable Western novels. Born in Kansas City, Missouri, Newton went on to complete work for a Master's degree in history at the University of Missouri. From the time he first discovered Max Brand in Street and Smith's *Western Story Magazine*, he knew he wanted to be an author of Western fiction. He began contributing Western stories and novelettes to the Red Circle group of Western pulp magazines published by Newsstand in the late 1930s. During the Second World War, Newton served in the US Army Engineers and fell in love with the central Oregon region when stationed there. He would later become a permanent resident of that state and Oregon frequently serves as the locale for many of his finest novels. As a client of the August Lenniger Literary Agency, Newton found that every time he switched publishers he was given a different byline by his agent. This complicated his visibility. Yet in notable novels from *Range Boss* (1949), the first original novel ever published in a modern paperback edition, through his impressive list of titles for the Double D series from Doubleday, *The Oregon Rifles, Crooked River Canyon*, and *Disaster Creek* among them, he produced a very special kind of Western story. What makes it so special is the combination of characters who seem real and about whom a reader comes to care a great deal and Newton's fundamental humanity, his realization early on (perhaps because of his study of history) that little that happened in the West was ever simple but rather made desperately complicated through the conjunction of numerous opposed forces working at cross purposes. Yet, through all of the turmoil on the frontier, a basic human decency did emerge. It was this which made the American frontier experience so profoundly unique and which produced many of the remarkable human beings to be found in the world of Newton's Western fiction.

THE RUTHLESS BREED

D. B. Newton

GUNSMOKE

This hardback edition 2008
by BBC Audiobooks Ltd
by arrangement with
Golden West Literary Agency

Copyright © 1966 by D. B. Newton.
All rights reserved.

ISBN 978 1 405 68156 8

British Library Cataloguing in Publication Data available.

Printed and bound in Great Britain by
Antony Rowe Ltd., Chippenham, Wiltshire

I

A subtle change in the rhythm of the engine's drive wheels roused Steve Benson and he came up out of a doze, blinking eyes that felt sandpapered. The train was climbing, sure enough, making slow grade; that meant they'd be on the long pull up to the summit of Dead Man, where they would pause to take on water and refuel from the high woodricks alongside the track. A look through dirtstreaked windowglass showed him the black silhouettes of tumbled rock and timber sliding by, and sliver of a moon in its last quarter. It was the dead, motionless hub of the night, with daylight no more than a few hours away.

In slightly more time than that, this trip would be over. Benson was train-weary, more than ready to have it over with.

He eased cramped muscles, trying in vain to fit himself to a seat that wasn't designed for anyone his size, and a town suit that couldn't fit itself to the breadth of his shoulders; rope-hardened fingers briefly touched the inside breast pocket of his coat, to check the safety of the envelope he carried there. By the dim light of turned-down lamps, he looked along the coach whose timbers creaked as the swaying walls warped in and out of shape. Tilted chairs and sprawled sleeping bodies stretched before him. He caught the sounds of snoring, smelled the mingled odors of coal oil and sweat, cigar smoke and soot and dusty plush upholstery.

Across the aisle a baby stirred, in the arms of the woman who sat alone there. It began a cranky whimpering and Benson watched as the woman roused herself and tried anxiously to comfort and settle it, before it could disturb the other passengers. He had been watching her, off and on, ever since the train left Denver; it seemed to Benson that her arms must be nearly ready to drop off by now, from fatigue. She was a little thing, with dark and worried eyes that, for some reason, bothered him. As he saw her push back the hair wearily from her forehead he wondered idly where her husband was. Waiting for her, he supposed, at one of the stations along the route.

A lucky man whoever he was, Steve Benson thought—without jealousy—because he had a girl of his own and didn't have to begrudge some other fellow a pretty wife, like that one just across the aisle. . . .

The train had gained the level of the pass and was creaking and grinding to a halt. A glimmer of lamplight in the watchman's shack slid past; up ahead the gaunt skeleton of a water tower showed in silhouette against the stars. As the coach settled, with a final lurch, passengers began to stir and waken. A drummer in the seat in front of Benson heaved himself around. "This a town?"

"Just a water stop. Next town's Coldbrook. Another couple hours at least."

A pair of trainmen paused below the window for a moment's routine talk, then walked on toward the front of the

6

train. Someone else, with a swaying lantern, passed along the line checking grease boxes; the night swallowed him.

The door at the forward end of the coach opened and Benson glanced up, idly, expecting to see the conductor. Instead, two men in range clothes and windbreakers had paused just within the entrance. Benson's attention was riveted as he caught what looked to be a glint of metal in the hand of one of them. Then the larger of the two raised his head and revealed the dark cloth tied across the lower portion of his face.

Steve Benson thought, *Holdup!* He had never heard of one on this unimportant feeder line; but there was always a first time, even for that. His hand moved unconsciously toward his leg before he remembered that, of course, he wasn't wearing his gun and rig in its accustomed place. He sat poised, his thoughts racing.

The big man spoke suddenly, in a voice that carried roughly through the folds of the mask: "All right, my friends! We're here to do a little business. Everybody mind what you're told and no one will get hurt!"

With that the car really came to life. There were startled outcries as passengers, still drugged by sleep, stumbled to their feet and then froze at sight of a pair of hand guns menacing them. The eyes above the big man's mask raked the car, but when they reached Steve Benson's face they stopped and held there boldly. Benson felt something tighten inside him.

He had an instinctive feeling that the man wasn't merely sizing up a job. He was hunting a particular target—and he'd found it.

Suddenly he was starting along the aisle, leaving his companion to guard the forward door. He paused a time or two, forcing a man to dig out a wallet which he dropped into a pocket of his windbreaker, ordering a woman to strip a ring from her finger. But Steve Benson was sure with every moment that this was only for effect. Quickly he slid a hand under his coat, slipped the manila envelope from his breast

7

pocket. He was casting about for a place to get rid of it—perhaps, between the cushion and the side of the seat—when he heard the woman whisper: "That's the first place he'd look. Quick! Give it to me!" He turned in surprise, saw her eyes, her outstretched hand.

He hesitated a moment, reluctant to involve her in this. But the approaching holdup man was for that moment occupied, and he could think of no better alternative. As he leaned to pass the envelope across the aisle, dim light of the ceiling lamp showed him what he hadn't noticed before: There was no answering gleam from that left hand she reached toward him. The woman wore no wedding ring.

He barely had time to register this, watching her deftly stowing the envelope away in the bundle in her arms. For now a shadow fell across Benson and he looked up into a masked face, and into the muzzle of a gun. Eyes as hard and round as nailheads peered at him from below the sweated brim of a downpulled hat. "Your turn!" the man said heavily.

He kept his own face carefully unrevealing. "You're wasting your time. I got nothing worth your trouble."

"I'll decide that! You pack a wallet, I reckon. Get it up—and don't try anything funny while you do it!"

Benson shrugged, reached toward a hip pocket. With those hard eyes watching his every movement, he dug out a worn billfold that was warped and badly sweatstained. He had scarcely got it clear when it was snatched from him. Awkwardly, onehanded—his other hand being filled with gunmetal—the big man thumbed the billfold open and revealed its contents, a few crumpled bills. He stared at these in silence, for a long moment.

Up forward, at the coach door, his companion called nervously: "Better hurry it!"

With a smothered curse, the man flung the billfold from him. His eyes lifted to his victim's face; the gunbarrel rose menacingly. "Don't fool with me!" he snapped tautly.

Benson returned the look, his face betraying nothing. "I

told you. You've just thrown away all you're going to find on me!"

The thick chest swelled on an angry breath. Then the big man gestured with the gunbarrel. "On your feet!"

Unhurriedly, Benson pushed to a stand. He seemed at ease, as though being held up at gunpoint was nothing to bother him. Actually he was inwardly tensed, his weight shifted slightly forward in his sharp-toed cattleman's boots.

Big as the masked bandit was, he topped Benson's rangy height by no more than an inch or two. "Raise your hands!" he ordered. "Stand hitched. . . ." Then, swiftly, he ran his free hand over Benson's clothing, checking his pockets. Finding nothing, he seemed to lose his temper. Suddenly he grabbed the front of Benson's shirt and gave a yank. Buttons popped loose and the shirt tail was pulled free. If he'd expected to find a money belt strapped to Benson's waist, under the shirt, he was again disappointed. The black brows pulled down fiercely, in what had the look of a baffled scowl.

"Satisfied?" Benson asked.

The bell on the engine began to sound, now.

The man at the door called in an anxious voice: "Hey! Come on! Train's starting to pull out. . . ."

The big man, ignoring the warning, lifted his head for a look at the luggage rack above the seats. Directly over Benson's head, a carpetbag rested. "That should be yours," the bandit said harshly. "Fetch it down, and let's have a look."

Benson could see puzzlement, now, beginning to mingle with the fear in the eyes of the other passengers as they saw the special treatment he was getting. He said nothing, and he took his time, lifting his shoulders in a shrug as he turned to reach for the carpetbag. And at that moment, the car gave a sudden lurch. Every person in the coach was thrown off balance, briefly; there was a squawk of alarm from the man at the door. Benson's guard had been sent staggering backward, bootheels reaching for solid footing.

It was the moment Steve Benson had been poised and ready for. As he saw the sixgun swing off target, he whirled

9

and let the movement of the car throw him straight at the other. He groped for a handhold on the gun, missed his try. Under the impetus of his lunge, he smashed full against the man's thick chest; then both of them were checked by the back of a seat across the aisle. Past his opponent's elbow Benson caught a glimpse of the woman, clutching her baby, and she was pale and wide-eyed with alarm.

With the cries of startled passengers in his ears, he swung at the face behind the mask but, lacking solid footing under him, his blow lacked steam. Next second he was trying desperately to fall away as he saw the gunbarrel streaking lamplight, in a downward arc aimed at his own head.

He fell to his knees in the aisle and the gunbarrel, barely grazing the side of his skull, landed with glancing force in the angle between neck and shoulder. He almost shouted with the pain. It was a paralyzing blow that left him crumpled, momentarily incapable of moving to protect himself or even of thinking clearly. But now, through the car floor, he could feel the wheels slowly grinding into motion. And at the forward door, the second bandit suddenly lost his nerve. "I'm gettin' out of here!" he cried in panic. The racket of the moving train came with suddenly increased loudness as the door was wrenched open.

The big man seemed to reach a decision, then. Benson heard him curse; painfully, he lifted his head and saw the bandit turn and start at a run back through the car, roughly shoving aside passengers who might have blocked his way. He reached the door, flung it open and was gone, leaving behind him a mounting hubbub of confusion.

Steve Benson grabbed a chair arm and hauled himself to his feet. The train was steadily gathering momentum; staggering a little, he got ahold of his carpetbag and dragged it off the rack, letting it drop to the seat. His teeth were set in pain but his movements were quick and purposeful as, working one-handed, he unsnapped the fastenings, fumbled inside the bag and from among its few contents of extra clothing brought out his gun and holster, with the shellbelt

10

wrapped around them. The gun was all he wanted. He snatched it free, shaking off the holster.

All this time his left arm, numbed by the blow, hung useless as if it had been broken.

Excitement was all around him. Someone tried to delay him with a hurried question but he pushed by, heading up the aisle. A voice cried suddenly, "There they go!" A man was crouching next to a window that had been run open, letting cold wind gust into the car. Quickly Benson shouldered him aside, thrust his own head and shoulders into the opening.

Earth and rocks and trees were beginning to wheel by with increasing speed in the elusive moonlight, as the train gathered momentum; but he caught a glimpse of a pair of horsemen, suddenly bursting out of a clump of trees and spurring off down a long slope studded with slant rock. He steadied his wrist on the window sill and squeezed off a couple of shots. Then the movement of the train carried him out of range and the escaping bandits had vanished.

The cold slip of night wind against face and chest helped clear some of the confusion from his thoughts. Slowly he drew back from the opening and straightened, holding the smoking gun. The one who had raised the window—a cowhand, in jeans and hickory shirt—asked quickly, "Did you get 'em?"

He shook his head. "Never even came close."

"What the hell do you think they were after? Damned if it didn't look like that big fellow had you singled out, the way he—"

But Steve Benson had already turned his back on his questioner.

II

THEY WERE GATHERING speed, now, as they took the downgrade on the far side of the pass; probably none of the train crew was even aware yet of the holdup attempt. As he

11

fought the sway of the coach, Steve Benson switched the smoking gun to his other hand and massaged that crippled left shoulder, that ached with a steady throbbing. He regained his seat and, standing beside it, dropped his gun into the carpetbag. He turned to look at the woman across the aisle.

The shouting and gunfire and the tumult in the narrow aisle had started the baby crying, and the woman was just managing to get it quieted again. She looked up at him, her face pale. "Are—are you hurt?" she asked in an unsteady voice.

Benson moved his shoulder, winced. He said, "I can still use it." He leaned and recovered the wallet that had been thrown aside. The woman meanwhile was groping in the folds of the blanket that wrapped the baby. She brought out the manila envelope and as she handed it to him their fingers met; hers felt quite cold. Benson looked at her hand and noticed again the absence of any sign of a gold band. He hoped she didn't think he was staring.

"Thanks a plenty for this," he said, taking the envelope. "I shouldn't have let you risk it. Maybe you can guess what might have happened if he'd seen."

"The envelope is what he was after?"

Benson nodded, but didn't elaborate as he put it back into his pocket. In so doing he was reminded of his ruined shirt. He made an effort to pull the remains together across his bare chest, and shove the shirttails home. But the woman scarcely appeared to notice. She was studying his face, looking up at him with a frown of thought.

"I have a feeling," she said suddenly, "that you knew who that man was. In spite of the mask."

Steve Benson returned her look for a long moment, before he nodded. His voice was crisp with angry emotion. "No mask can really hide a man, or change the sound of his voice. Yeah—I knew who it was!"

Then, abruptly, with the air of a man who had answered all the questions he meant to, he turned away and started

12

digging in his carpetbag for a new shirt. The woman watched him, frowning a little, and patting the baby with that ringless left hand.

Daylight was an hour old when Steve Benson noticed that, instead of merely finding the view from the coach window generally familiar, he now recognized every outline of hill and jutting rock along the right of way. The train, having snaked its way down from the pass, had descended into rangeland—a broad valley, cupped by long-running, pineclad hills and the granite peaks of farther mountains. The railroad merely touched the lower end of this valley, before working its way again into the hills. But there was a town here; and before the conductor came through the car announcing, "Coldbrook—next stop!" Benson was already on his feet and reaching his carpetbag down off the rack.

As the brakes began to grab and the engine's whistle sent its voice echoing off the timbered rises, he stood in the vestibule between the cars with metal floorplates shuddering underfoot. Empty corrals and loading chutes went by, and the first scattered shacks; and then the ugly clapboard station was sliding toward him, with baggage trucks on the high platform, and the station agent waiting with mailbag and clipboard. The early sun flashing off windowglass stabbed at his eyes, and he pulled his hatbrim lower.

Despite the importance of his mission, and a sense of excitement at seeing it completed over the last-minute obstacle of an attempted holdup, he found he was still thinking chiefly of that girl in the day coach. He could still picture how she'd looked as he stopped a moment to say good-bye— the baby asleep in her arms, valley floor wheeling past the window behind her, morning sunlight outlining the curve of her cheek and finding a gleam of copper in her dark hair above it.

It was in no way his concern, but he knew she would continue to trouble him. He would long remember the pathetic look of that hand without a wedding ring, and the

13

thing he had come to sense in her—the feeling that here was someone steeling herself to an ordeal that awaited her, wherever it was she was going. . . .

As he swung down off the still-moving coach steps, Benson saw a man straighten from a lean against the front of the depot where he had been waiting, his breath making a fog in the early chill. A stocky, blunt-faced man of forty, with thinning sandy hair and a perpetually serious manner, Joe Niles came forward to meet his partner. He said without preliminary, "I got your telegram. We're all set?"

Benson nodded; but he said, "Looks like you're not the only one got the news."

"What do you mean?"

"Burke Sully and some other fellow boarded the train at Dead Man Summit. Gave me a little surprise welcome."

Niles stared. "The hell they did! You mean, stuck you up?"

Benson nodded. "A real Jesse James performance. Masks and everything." He called his partner's attention to the conductor and the station agent, excitedly talking. The latter turned and gave an order to someone that sent him hurrying off. "Going for the sheriff," Benson guessed.

Joe Niles could think of only one thing. He asked sharply, "They didn't get it, did they?"

"No—they didn't get it; I was lucky. The way they acted, they seemed to think I'd have been fool enough to carry all that on me, in cash."

The older man rubbed a hand across his broad cheeks, pulling his mouth out of shape. "I knew Wes Coldbrook would do almost anything to stop this deal—but even he don't seem fool enough to try a thing like that! You're positive it was Burke Sully? No chance of a mistake?"

"No mistake. A piece of cloth over his face isn't going to hide the size of a man like Sully—or disguise his voice, either."

"What about the other one?"

14

"I didn't get much of a look at him," Benson admitted. "Sully kept me too busy."

Another thought had crossed his partner's rather slow mind. "How you reckon they knew you'd be on this train? Have the Coldbrooks got spies workin' in Denver?"

Benson shook his head. "They wouldn't need them. More likely they know what's in any telegraph message that goes in or out of town. Mine only said, 'I have the money.' That might give Wes the idea I was bringing it in cash."

Joe Niles stiffened. "You really think that damned brass pounder—?" He swung angrily toward the telegrapher's window, but Benson grabbed his arm.

"Cool off! It might only have been a coincidence—it was no secret, why I went to Denver. Anyway, it doesn't matter. The important thing is that it didn't work this time." He touched a pocket of his coat. "The money's safe, and nothing to stop us going out to Gannon's place and closing our deal."

Joe Niles, still scowling, agreed: "Yeah—before the old guy changes his mind."

"I don't think he's going to do that."

"Wes Coldbrook seems to think he can be persuaded."

"Then he doesn't know Abel Gannon. . . . You had breakfast?"

"No."

"Neither have I. We'll stop in at Mike's for something, and then get our horses and—"

He broke off in surprise. The train was just now whistling into motion again. As it pulled ponderously away, Steve Benson saw the young woman standing alone on the platform with the baby in her arms, and a couple of suitcases at her feet. The shadows of the cars flickered over her; then the train was gone, its noise dying along the steel rails at their feet, and the woman was left full in the thin morning sunlight. She looked small and very much alone.

Joe Niles saw the direction of his partner's frown. "Somebody you know?"

"Just a minute."

15

Benson left him and walked over to the woman. As she heard his step on the cinders she turned quickly; seeing who it was she said, "Oh—hello, again."

He touched his hatbrim. "Was someone supposed to be meeting you?"

"No. Nobody." He thought she seemed frightened and ill at ease, fumbling with the baby's blanket to shield him from the crisp morning. "Could you tell me, is there a hotel or—"

"A hotel? We got a good one here—*The Coldbrook House.* It's brand-new—Troy Coldbrook built it himself." Quickly he leaned to get her luggage. "Let me show you. It's only a couple of blocks."

"I wouldn't want to bother you. . . ."

"You couldn't bother me," he told her flatly. "Not after what you did last night!" He turned and jerked his head at Joe Niles, who was watching this in plain puzzlement. "Joe," he said, "I'm seeing this young lady to the hotel. Take care of my bag for me, and I'll meet you at Mike's as soon as she's taken care of."

The smaller man sounded dubious. "Don't be too long. Now we're this close to winding this business up, I'm getting a little anxious."

The woman must have caught the urgency in his voice. "I know I'm being a nuisance. . . ."

"Not at all," Benson said. Joe Niles stepped aside, nodding as the young woman gave him an uncertain smile. He stood watching the two of them move down the station platform and around the corner.

Benson said, "You never told me you were getting off here at Coldbrook."

"You never asked me."

"I guess that's right, at that. Maybe I ought to introduce myself." He told his name, adding, "That funnylooking little guy at the depot was my partner."

"Business partner?"

"We're equal shares in a shirttail cattle ranch, over on the

16

edge of the flats. We'll never steal Troy Coldbrook's thunder, but we're not all that ambitious."

He felt her eyes on his face, searching it with a frowning intentness. "Troy Coldbrook, again. That's twice I've heard you mention him, as though he must be someone pretty important. Did they name the town for him?"

"Why not? It's his town!" Perhaps she caught the edge of sourness in his voice; she didn't question further. It was a minute or so before it occurred to Benson that she hadn't offered him her name, in acknowledgement of his own.

The dusty main street stretched away a distance of four long blocks from the depot, with a vista of timbered hills and granite peaks lifting above the rooftops. Benson escorted the young woman across the station plaza and so to the cement sidewalk along the street's northern side. Morning sunlight beating off the brick fronts of store-buildings took away some of the chill of the early season.

They passed a livery stable and a saloon and a feed store and then, as the tone of the street began to improve, the bank with its wooden Grecian pillars, painted white. Beyond the second street crossing the hotel showed, a big corner building with deep verandas running along its two fronts, and a line of wooden rocking chairs tilted against the deserted porch railings.

A couple of Coldbrook punchers were loafing in front of the hardware store, apparently waiting for it to open. Vic Gilmore, a loose-coupled man with a pale stare and a vacuous, thin-lipped grin, nudged his companion as he eyed the woman and her blanket-wrapped burden. His bold stare sought Steve Benson's face then and his grin widened. "That's what I call fast work, Steve," he said, with ruttish humor. "You was only gone a week!" He laughed loudly at his own joke.

Benson's mouth pulled tight and he nearly halted in his tracks. But he thought better of it and as he walked on, holding onto his temper, Vic Gilmore's laugh followed him. A glance at the woman showed him she was staring straight

17

ahead of her, but the cheek that he could see was fiery red. Benson gritted his teeth and said nothing, and neither did she.

They crossed at the side street, mounted the wide corner steps to the hotel veranda, under the swaying sign; Benson set down one of the bags while he opened the door and let the woman enter ahead of him. The lobby was deserted—a bright, sunny place with a look of newness about it.

There were potted rubber plants, comfortable chairs upholstered in leather, a carpet on the stairs that had yet to be defaced by trailing spurs. Steve Benson thought *Coldbrook House* compared favorably with the hotel he'd stayed in during his trip to Denver; he had to pay Troy Coldbrook that much of a compliment, however grudgingly.

Still, if old Troy had spent money lavishly in fitting out his hotel, he undoubtedly was figuring to get it back again from his customers—with interest.

A touch of Benson's calloused finger on the desk bell brought the manager—a bustling little man who rubbed his palms together and beamed nervously at sight of an attractive young woman. "Just off the train, George," Benson told him. "She needs a room. Fix her up, will you?"

"More than happy to." George Meeks opened the register and turned it for her signature. "How long will you be with us?"

She shifted the sleeping baby onto her left arm as she picked up the pen. "I don't really know. So I'll take it for a week. . . ."

Steve Benson didn't mean to pry but he still caught a glimpse, across her shoulder, of what she wrote: "Miss Ruth Faris, Denver." The manager was still smiling as he turned the register again. "I have a very nice one on the second floor, front, Mrs.—" His eye sought the name. His smile faltered very slightly. "*Miss* Faris."

Suddenly his busy glance, behind polished lenses, couldn't seem to settle; it flicked uneasily to the woman's face, to the baby, to Steve Benson looming beside her. He turned away,

18

abruptly, to fumble a key from the board next to the letter rack; watching him, Benson had considerable trouble hiding his exasperation.

Benson pulled off his hat as he said, more gruffly than he meant to, "I have to go—my partner's waiting. I hope you'll be comfortable here."

"I'm sure I will. Thank you ever so much, Mr. Benson." She offered her hand. It was small, hard and firm—a hand plainly used to hard work. He held it briefly, and then turned and walked out of the hotel.

Ruth Faris was still looking at the closed door when the manager coughed slightly. "Uh—that'll be fourteen dollars, for the week."

"Oh—yes, of course." As she got the money out of her reticule, awkwardly because of her burden, she asked, "I wonder if I could have some milk warmed for the baby."

"I'll have it sent right up." He swept her money into a cash drawer below the desk, afterward lifting the drop leaf and coming around to get her bags. Ruth Faris hesitated, suddenly asked, "And—can you tell me where I'd be apt to find Mr. Coldbrook."

He looked at her quickly. "Troy Coldbrook?"

"Yes," she said. "I—I suppose that's who I want."

"Why, far as I know he'd be at the ranch. He hasn't been home but a day or two. Him and Miz Coldbrook just got back from a trip. To Europe, no less. Paris, and Rome—all them countries."

"How far would it be to his ranch?"

"Keystone? Some fifteen miles, I guess, up the valley road. Anybody could tell you—it's the biggest around here." He couldn't keep from asking, "You got business with Mr. Coldbrook? Kin of his, maybe?"

"No," she said quickly. "No kin." She evidently had no more to say. George Meeks had to swallow his curiosity as he took her bags, and started for the carpeted stairway ahead of her.

19

Steve Benson was in a poor mood as he swung down the veranda steps and into morning sunlight, retracing his course toward the depot. Vic Gilmore and the other Coldbrook hand still waited outside the hardware store; they broke off their talk and watched him go by in silence. From a corner of his eye Benson saw once more the grin on Gilmore's face. It hit with a delayed force.

He had taken a couple of further steps when suddenly his jaw set hard, and he pivoted sharply on one heel. A solid stride brought him back, face to face with Gilmore; the latter tried to back away, alarm touching his slack features as he saw the glint in Benson's eye. Gilmore's hands came up, belatedly. Benson brushed them aside and his right fist came over, a hard jolting swing of bunched knuckles that caught Gilmore's flush on the point of the jaw.

Gilmore's head jarred back on his shoulders. He was driven back, a half dozen short steps, before his heel caught on the edge of the sidewalk and he went to a sitting position in the street ruts with dry dust whooshing out from under him. He sat there, dazed, and Steve Benson turned away shaking his tingling knuckles with a real sense of satisfaction. He left the second Coldbrook puncher staring after him in startled surprise, before the man turned to see what he could do for his fallen companion.

There had been something quite satisfying in the look of complete surprise on Vic Gilmore's face—the look of a man who hadn't been expecting to have his crude attempt at a joke knocked back between his teeth. As far as Benson was concerned, it was the only really pleasant experience he had had since Burke Sully boarded the train at Dead Man. He had had just about enough of anything and everything connected with the name of Coldbrook.

III

A MOUNTED MAN waited for him at the eat shack, a gaunt figure with a black waterfall of mustache, sitting hipshot in the saddle with a rifle thrusting from the scabbard under his knee. Sunlight flashed from the metal shield pinned to his coat. "Hello, Benson," he said.

Benson nodded carefully. "Morning, Sheriff."

Without preliminary, Tom Fawcett said, "Train conductor was telling me you ran into a little trouble up at Dead Man."

"That's right. Somebody tried a stickup."

"It's in my county, so I guess I'm going to have to get out there and look around for horse sign. Wanted to find out first, is there anything you can add to what I already know?"

"Nothing, besides what I told the conductor when he questioned me. There was a pair of them. A whole carfull of people saw what happened."

The sheriff nodded. He stroked his silky mustache with thumb and forefinger; his eyes were blank and careful. "From what I hear, they kind of seem to have singled you out."

"Don't know any reason why they should do that. They certainly didn't get anything from me."

"You don't maybe have some clue as to who they were?"

For just a moment Benson weighed his answer, debating whether to talk frankly. As far as he knew Sheriff Fawcett was a fair man—an honest officer. Yet to be a sheriff in Troy Coldbrook's county meant, of necessity, being a special protector of Coldbrook interests. To name Coldbrook's foreman, without definite proof, seemed useless and perhaps even risky; Benson shook his head. He said, "They both were masked."

A pause. Then the sheriff shrugged and lifted the reins, straightening as he slogged a boot into the stirrup. "No harm asking. God knows I got little enough to go on. Thanks anyway."

"Sure," Steve Benson said, and as the lawman rode slowly away through morning sunlight he turned and walked into the eat shack.

The very air seemed to swim with grease. Joe Niles, on a counter stool, was already half finished with his breakfast. "Get the little lady fixed up?" he asked, as his partner hung up his hat and took the adjoining stool. His tone revealed that he was fairly eaten up with curiosity that was only poorly concealed.

Before answering, Benson turned to the man behind the counter and indicated his partner's plate of fried eggs, potatoes, bacon. "Give me the same. But first, a cup of coffee." Joe Niles waited in silence; if he noticed the split skin over the knuckles of the hand with which his partner stirred sugar and cream into his coffee, he said nothing.

But Steve Benson could read his partner like a book, and when the silence became too pointed he said, as he set his cup down half-empty, "For your information—and to set that suspicious mind of yours at rest—I was returning a favor. Happens, that young woman was the reason Burke Sully didn't get away with what he tried last night." Briefly he told of her presence of mind in offering to take the envelope and hide it. "She did it right under his nose, without having any idea of what was in it—or what he might do if he saw her."

Joe Niles listened soberly. "That took nerve," he agreed. "I get the chance, I'd like to thank her myself."

Benson waited until the cook had brought him a steaming plate of food and returned to his sink of dirty dishes. "Everything's in here. The bank in Denver had a lawyer draw up papers for me, so there's nothing to it except a matter of a couple of signatures, and then giving Abel Gannon the bank draft made out in his name. Then the deal's closed."

"Good enough," the older man said. "So let's go out there and close it. I keep thinking something else can go wrong."

"Nothing has yet. Not really."

"Just the same, you better take good care of that envelope. They've tried once to get it."

"They won't catch me napping again," Benson promised grimly, and returned it to his pocket.

But the other man was uneasy, and he bolted down the rest of his breakfast and drained his second cup of coffee, drummed rope-tough fingers on the counter impatiently as he watched his companion. "I got a pair of horses at the livery," he said. "It'll save time if I go saddle, while you're finishing there."

"All right." He added, "Don't suppose you happened to think to bring me along a change of clothes?"

Niles looked at the ill-fitting suit. "Happens I did. I figured you wouldn't want to ride far, in them duds you got on. You'd split out the pants, after ten minutes in a saddle." He slid off his stool, leaned for the carpetbag. "Want me to take this?"

"You might as well. I've got one more call to make before I can leave."

"*Another* one?" Niles gave him a sour look. "What is it this time—business, or social?"

"It's social," Benson said, and grinned at the other's expression. "But don't get in an uproar. I'll only be a minute. . . ."

Pausing outside the eat shack a little later, he checked the time on the watch from his pocket. It was just past eight—too early, actually, to be calling on Laurel Whitney; but he had a present for her in his pocket and he couldn't be sure when he would have another opportunity to see her and give it to her. He rather hoped he wouldn't run into her father. It might be embarrassing, this of all mornings.

Dan Whitney was the cause of Benson being forced to go clear to Denver to arrange his loan, since Dan had turned down his original attempt to borrow what he needed. It wasn't very smart of course, in the first place, applying at a bank Troy Coldbrook owned a big piece of for a loan to buy property the Coldbrooks wanted. Even so, because of

Laurel, Benson had thought Dan Whitney might seriously consider his proposition. Instead, the whole thing had turned out unpleasantly, with Dan forced to think up spurious reasons for refusing when they both, after all, knew what the true reasons were.

The Coldbrooks: Their influence seemed to hang over this town and this country like a cloud. . . .

He turned back up the street, to the corner where the bank stood with its doors still locked and the curtains pulled on the big windows; here he turned up the hill toward the big house on the next street over. Dan Whitney had built himself a real palace—milled lumber, two stories of it, all bow windows and gingerbread and deep verandas. It sat well back, with a wide lawn and a fence surrounding it and a cast iron stag on the watch for huntsmen. Steve Benson, always a little ill at ease for all the times he had been here, followed the curving walk and climbed the wide front steps. He took a moment to settle the hang of his coat and nervously straighten his string tie. Afterward he turned the bell handle in the middle of the front door.

He waited. The door opened a crack and the Whitney's housekeeper peered out at him, frowning with disapproval. "Ain't this a little early for paying calls, Mr. Benson?" she said.

"I just got off the morning train, in from Denver," he explained. "I'd like to see Miss Whitney, if it's at all possible."

The woman started to grumble but a clear young voice from behind her interrupted. "It's all right, Martha." Still scowling the woman backed away, and through the widening door Steve Benson saw the blue-eyed girl standing on the wide stairway that curved toward the upper floor. He pulled off his hat and stepped across the threshold as Laurel came down the last few steps, skirts and blonde curls dancing. As the housekeeper closed the door and waddled off down the hall, Laurel caught Benson's arm and drew him toward a tasseled doorway. "Come in here," she said.

He had always found the Whitney parlor a bit overpowering, with its heavy dark furniture and thick carpeting and heavy velvet drapes, in the latest elegant style. There were plants and ostrich feathers and a stuffed bird under glass. In the big stone fireplace, behind massive andirons, a log fire was crackling—the only cheery thing about the room, except for Laurel Whitney herself. Though she was twenty, she seemed almost like a child as she stood before him in the middle of this museum to her father's prosperity—a gay and teasing child, capable of charming him utterly, even when nearly every other word she spoke irritated him at the plain evidence of the shameless way her father had spoiled her.

He felt like spanking her sometimes. Usually—as right now, in the pleasure of seeing her again after a week's absence—he had to restrain himself to keep from sweeping her hungrily into his arms. This mausoleum of a parlor scarcely seemed the right place for that, so he merely bent and brushed her forehead with his lips. "Now!" she said, as he straightened. "What did you bring me from Denver?"

"What made you think I brought you anything?"

For a moment he was almost a little put out with her. He had invested a lot of thought and anticipation in his gift, thinking to surprise her; this apparent taking it for granted somehow dulled the edge of his pleasure. But he smiled a little, ruefully, wondering after all what he could have expected? Without these little traits of innocent selfishness, she somehow wouldn't have been Laurel Whitney.

With a shrug he reached into his coat pocket and brought out a small box tied with ribbon. She almost snatched it from him, and spun away to open it in the better light of one of the deeply curtained windows. When she saw the brooch and matching earrings, of red coral mounted on gold, she let out a squeal of delight. "Oh, they're beautiful! How did you know they were just what I'd like?"

"I didn't," he admitted. "I had to guess. I don't know much about such things. But—you *do* like them?"

"Of course!" She whirled to him, hugged and kissed him

25

on the cheek, rising impulsively on tiptoe to do it. His slight sense of pique was mollified; he let her take him by the hand and lead him to a seat on the ugly horsehair sofa. She set the box on a table and said, "I want to know all the news of Denver!"

"I was only in town five days," he pointed out. "Afraid I didn't see anything much except my hotel room and the banker's office. Sorry."

Perfect, winged brows drew down as she frowned at him, uncomprehendingly. "Five whole days! And you never took time to go to any of the stores, or—or go to the theater, or anything?"

He looked into those perplexed blue eyes and didn't know how to answer her. "I reckon that sort of thing's out of my line," he confessed lamely. "Besides, I was there on business—strictly. By the way," he added, "I got the loan I went for. I'm all set to finish the deal my friend and I have set up with old Abel Gannon. And that's why I can't stay and talk to you any longer, right now. Joe Niles is waiting to go out and get Gannon's signature on the papers."

Her full lips pouted. "You mean, you're going to run off and leave me all alone, just for a nasty old man like Abel Gannon?"

"Now, you know you shouldn't say that!" he reproved her, gently. "In the first place, he's not a nasty old man—even if he is sort of unpredictable and crossgrained at times. Since he lost his wife in that flash flood, last spring, he's seemed to me nothing but pathetic. She was all he had; now the only thing he can think about is selling out his property and getting out of a country that holds too many memories.

"And that's why it's important that Joe and I hurry out there, and put a binder on the deal we have with him. Can't you see what this can mean for us, and for the other small-scale ranchers on the flats? When we have control of Gannon's property, and his range rights, it means more than doubling our winter graze. It means every outfit in the Pool can increase his herds, take on extra crew." He reached suddenly, took Laurel Whitney's soft hand in his rope-scarred one. "It brings the day closer when I can start seriously planning for us, Laurel!"

He realized suddenly that she wasn't listening; she was off on a sudden new tangent of her own, that threw him completely off his guard as the girl demanded, her shoulders stiffening, "Who was she, Steven?"

Benson stopped talking, blinking a little as he tried to follow her sudden diverging thought. "She? Who do you mean?"

"You know who I mean!" Angrily, the girl jerked her fingers away from his, clasped both hands primly in her lap. Prettily stern, she said, "I saw you both, from my window upstairs. Looked to me like you were carrying her suitcases."

"Oh. Her." He understood, and he was distinctly flattered to detect a note of jealousy in her voice. "That was just a woman on the train. Perhaps you noticed, she was carrying a baby. I simply helped her as far as the hotel."

"Very gallant!" Laurel Whitney said, with a sniff. "Here *I* was, waiting for you. And there *you* were spending the whole morning with some strange woman, and—and goodness knows what all! Who is she, anyway?"

Steve Benson felt exasperation tighten his jaw muscles a little. "You're being ridiculous! She's a perfect stranger. I believe her name is Faris; what her business might be I haven't the slightest idea, because I didn't ask. As for where I spent the past hour since train time," he went on grimly, "I was at the eat shack with Joe Niles, having myself some breakfast and waiting until I thought it was a decent hour to come calling.

"And now," he added, swinging abruptly to his feet, "I'm afraid I've got to go. Joe's waiting and the day isn't getting any younger."

She rose quickly, her manner contrite as she put her hands in his. "I'm sorry! Oh, Steven! Why do we always seem to end up quarreling?"

"I don't know," he admitted frankly, looking down at her. "Doesn't make much sense, does it?"

"You know I missed you," she said. "It's been so dull around here. Absolutely nothing happening, except the dance at the Odd Fellows' hall Saturday night—Wes Coldbrook took me. Oh, and did you hear? Troy and Ada are back from Europe. They got home day before yesterday."

He nodded. "I know. Joe told me. Look, I really must—"

"All right." She added earnestly, "I *do* thank you for the present. And I really didn't mean what I said about that— that woman. Why, if she set her cap for you I bet you probably wouldn't even know it!"

He had to smile. "Okay," he said. "No more quarreling." When he bent to kiss her, she lifted her lips but something made him kiss her on the forehead again, instead. He didn't know why he should still feel a certain reserve toward her, as he picked his hat off the table where he had laid it and turned to the hall doorway. "Say hello to your father, for me."

"When will I see you again?"

"Afraid I can't tell you that. There's a lot waiting to do. I'll get in when I can. . . ."

With the big door closed behind him, he stood a moment filling his lungs as he frowned to himself. The day was turning warmer, his breath no longer making a mist in the clean air. White bands of frost still marked the shadows of the trees and fence pickets, but these would soon vanish as the warming sun hit them.

All too often, he was thinking, his moments with Laurel Whitney left him dissatisfied and wondering. He wished he understood her; he wished he understood himself. That she was thoroughly spoiled, he knew very well—but that was her father's doing. She was still young; she would outgrow it. And yet—

Wasn't she old enough now, that some of this immaturity should begin to wear off? It was a great part of her charm, of her strong appeal for him that sometimes filled him with

28

such an overwhelming hunger that it almost frightened him; but again it irritated him, and sent him away sometimes wondering how he put up with her willful unconcern for any feelings except her own. . . .

It was too big a problem. He shook his head at it, pulling on his hat as he started for the livery where Joe Niles would be waiting and, no doubt, fuming over the delay.

IV

THE BUILDING WAS a one-room shack, of mud-daubed pole construction with a sagging shake roof, that Keystone used for a line camp when it had beef up here in the hills on summer range. Now it was out of use and the rock chimney had a cold look, no smoke rising from it. But there were a pair of horses in the corral adjoining, and these lifted their heads and pricked their ears as the two riders came down out of the timber.

Early morning sun was drawing fingers of steam from the meadow before the shack, giving a golden sheen to the pines along the clearing. But Burke Sully saw no beauty in the morning. He was dogtired, chilled to the bone, and short of temper because of last night's fiasco. There was a sore place in the corner of his mouth, split by the glancing blow of Steve Benson's fist, and his tongue couldn't leave it alone; he probed at it and tasted blood, and swore under his breath.

In a heavy silence, that had held for most of the time since the fizzle of the holdup attempt at Dead Man, the two tired men reined up before the cabin and swung stiffly down. Sully turned immediately to the task of stripping saddle and gear from the knotheaded bay he had ridden to Dead Man. He set the animal loose, and lugged the heavy stock saddle over to the pen where the black gelding that was his personal first-string mount waited. Part of the planning of last night's affair had been to bring extra horses with them as far as this line shack, in order to avoid a risk of having their own saddlers seen and recognized, and to have a fresh remount ready and waiting if anything went wrong and they needed it.

Wes Coldbrook, watching Sully work with the gelding, called over: "When you get through switching saddles, you can take care of mine."

The other man stiffened; he turned and gave his companion a stabbing glance, full of rancor. "Take care of your own damn saddle!"

Young Coldbrook might as well have been slapped. His head jerked and a stain of color moved up through his cheeks to the roots of his tawny hair. He was a slim young fellow, this heir to the powerful Keystone brand—good-looking, in a pale-eyed, full-lipped way that gave him always a hint of a pouting expression. There was more than a hint of vanity in the way he wore his taffy-colored sideburns trimmed to scimitar points across smooth cheeks.

He looked at Burke Sully and he held back the angry retort that came to his tongue. Instead he said coldly, "You want to fix breakfast, instead? Take your pick—because I want something in my belly before I ride any farther."

"I want more than that," Sully answered. "I figure on some time on one of them bunks, inside there. I'm bushed!" There had been hours in the saddle for them both, in the ride to Dead Man and back, and no rest except for an uneasy nap while they waited for the train to arrive.

Wes Coldbrook told the foreman, "We're not through with this job yet. If you hadn't messed it up last night, and got that money from Benson like you were supposed to—it could have been different."

Sully's broad face turned ugly; his hard black eyes narrowed. "Let's keep the record straight, boy! *You* figured out that play, and a pretty dumb one it was, too! You handed me the tough part of it—all you had to do was stand by and give me cover. And then you lost your nerve and ran out on me!"

30

"Don't forget who you're talking to!" the young man cried, stung. His hands had begun trembling and he clenched them. "You could find yourself without a job!"

"Who's gonna fire me?" the other retorted, and gave a snort. "You? Try it and I'll knock the pudding out of you! Or maybe," he added, "you think old Troy Coldbrook will get rid of the best foreman he ever had—just because you ask him to! Hell, your pa's not *that* kind of a fool! He knows Keystone wouldn't last a month without me. Maybe he did go off and leave you in charge for a year, but only because he knew I was on hand to see to things!"

"That's a damned lie!" Wes Coldbrook retorted, turning red to the roots of his hair. "Any day you want to draw your time—" He let it trail off, evidently seeing from the mocking tightness of Sully's grin that the latter knew it for a bluff. He ended loudly, "Until then, watch your tongue. Get those saddles switched, and as soon as we've had some grub we're riding again."

The big man made no move. With his saddle at his feet and his thumbs hung in his shell belt, he said flatly, "If this is another notion as good as the one we tried last night, I want to know first where I'm riding!"

Young Coldbrook's jaw muscles bunched beneath the smooth cheeks; his fingers worked, clenching and unclenching.

"Maybe you think I'm lowering my sights on that place of Abel Gannon's," he said harshly, "just because last night turned out a bust. Long as no money's changed hands—and until Benson's name is on the deed—there's still time. We're going out there and we're giving the old fool one last chance to change his mind."

Burke Sully pointed out, "He's going to want cash. Where you expect to get it? From your pa?"

"No! This is *my* deal! I was hoping to have it settled before he got home; but, that's all right. He'll know just what I'm worth, when I hand him Gannon's grass on a platter."

31

"And, the money?" Sully repeated with maddening insistence.

"I'll get it from Dan Whitney, of course. All it took was a word from me to make him turn Benson down, after Laurel told me the guy was figuring to touch him for a loan. He'll be glad enough to put up the backing for any deal I can set up with Gannon."

"I dunno," the foreman said dubiously. "You don't look out, you're gonna play hell! That old bastard is stubborn. He ain't Dan Whitney—he's got no girl he wants to marry off to the Coldbrooks; he's not going to jump through any hoops, just to suit some crazy notion you've got in your head!" He added, "I still don't see what the hell you want with Gannon's spread. Keystone's more than you'll ever be able to handle."

"I'll have that range!" the other said tightly, a feverish gleam touching his stare. "I *got* to have it! And none of your damned business why!"

"And, Steve Benson? He's no fool. Even if he ain't guessed already who it was jumped him last night, once he sees you bidding against him he's going to start adding things—real fast! And I for one don't want him on *my* trail!"

"Benson!" Coldbrook said the name as though it were a bad word. "Who the hell is he—God, or somebody? He thinks he's really putting something over, with this deal of his. Well, I'll tell you right now: There ain't ever been but room for one big man in this country. Once it was Pa; now it's gonna be me. Not Benson, you understand? *Me!*"

The foreman looked at him askance, a purely dubious expression. He thought, but didn't say, *Just who is it you're trying to impress? Your pa who's cast a shadow you'll never escape from? Or that empty-headed Laurel Whitney, that dangles Steve Benson to keep you on the string? Or—your own pitiful, damned self?*

He shrugged, keeping these thoughts to himself. All he said was, "Whatever you do, you better do it fast. You don't know how long it's going to take Benson to get out to

Gannon's and settle things with him—but you can't count on much time."

"Then quit arguing, and change those saddles. I'll be throwing something together for us to eat. We can eat while we ride. . . ."

Abel Gannon had built his headquarters close to the eastern edge of the valley, where tall firs marched down the flank of the steep valley wall. The morning sun, halfway up the sky now, was just striking the ranch buildings where they sat in the shadow of the ridge. They were in fair condition, even though continuing bad fortune had forced Gannon to lay off the last of his crew, long months past. Smoke rose from the rock-and-daub chimney, spiraling up into yellowing sunlight. There were a couple of horses in the pen, but no saddled mounts tied at the feedlot. Young Coldbrook pointed this out to Burke Sully with a triumphant look, as they drew rein in a clump of second growth pine. "You see? We beat Benson here."

The other man made no answer. They rode on down out of the timber, into the yard.

A hound dog, chained at the side of the house, got their scent and began to jerk at his tether and raise a racket in the morning stillness. The door of the main house opened and an old man appeared, to watch his visitors pull up at the corral and dismount. He stood unmoving, with the morning breeze plucking at thinning hair, as the pair tied their horses to the bars and then approached the house, Wes Coldbrook in the lead. Abel Gannon's faded blue stare held no welcome; his mouth was tight-drawn and suspicious.

He lifted his voice, sharply: "I got no business with you, Wes Coldbrook. So you two might as well get back on your horses."

They kept walking, to reach a stand before the old man in the doorway. "Why, now," Wes said pleasantly, "that ain't no way to talk to a neighbor. Me and Burke was riding

33

range, and we thought there'd be no harm stopping by for a cup of coffee. Air's got a real nip to it this morning."

Shaggy brows lowered, old Gannon stared at him a long moment before the demands of common range courtesy got the better of his continuing suspicion. "Come in, then," he said reluctantly. "I got some on the stove."

The pair followed him into the warmth of the kitchen, and Sully quietly closed the door with his heel as Gannon hobbled over to the stove—a tortuous, crippled gait, that drew Coldbrook's stare with an eerie fascination. The smashed leg was an old injury, resulting from a riding accident. It had never actually healed; for twenty years or more Abel Gannon had fought it, thinking he was well, from time to time, only to have the infection break out again. And all his life Wes Coldbrook had found himself fascinated by the sight of the leg and the limp—wondering what sort of twisted horror it must be, inside the worn boot and shapeless trouser leg. . . .

Gannon put out a couple of heavy china cups on the scrubbed deal table, filled them from a battered metal coffeepot and set the pot back on the stove. He produced a tin filled with sugar, a can of evaporated milk, a couple of spoons. He looked at his guests, and a keener suspicion brightened his stare as he saw that neither of them had made any move toward the coffee.

"Well, there it is," he said. "If it's what you came for. Or—was it?" he added dryly.

Wes Coldbrook walked over, picked up one of the coffee cups and took a swallow. "All right, I'll quit beating around the bush. I come to tell you, for the last time, you're selling me this place of yours."

"Then you wasted your time, sonny. I already made it plain enough—my deal is with Steve Benson."

"I'll raise whatever price you've been offered."

The old man slowly wagged his head. "Troy Coldbrook ain't really a bad fellow," he said sourly, "but he sure as hell raised him a spoiled brat for a son! For all his money, I

34

never envied him but two things—a pair of straight legs, and a son to carry on his line. I buried both my own boys, before they was into their teens." He flung out an arm, pointing with his thumb toward a flyblown windowpane and the hill beyond, where a little cluster of graves lay under their neat crosses. "But I can't see that Troy ended up a hell of a lot better off!

"And he's only got himself to blame. He went and raised you all wrong—brought you up thinking you could have anything you want, just by offerin' a little more money than the next feller's got. Maybe your way works pretty good, too, up to a point. Ain't much question in my mind which of you is gonna end up with the girl you and Benson both want—that little snip of a banker's daughter. . . .

"But for your information, this here is one time when your way don't buy a thing!"

There was silence, for a moment. Angry color tinged the young man's cheeks and his hand had begun to shake until he had to set down the cup. "All right," he said harshly. "You don't have to like me. But I figure I got a right to know why Coldbrook money ain't at least as good as some greasy-sack cowman's."

The old man swallowed a retort. "That may be a fair question," he admitted, "since it all could have worked out different if Troy Coldbrook had been home last spring instead of off gallivantin' around Europe, and you in charge of Keystone. If Troy'd been here and got wind of what happened in that flash flood in Jawbone Canyon, he'd have been curious enough at least to want to know how an old friend was making out. Instead, it was left for Steve Benson to come around and find me all alone here, half dead from exposure and trying to finish the job with likker.

"He saved my life, Coldbrook! He neglected his own chores to do it. He not only pulled me through the pneumonia I got after that drowning, but he talked me out of giving up. I couldn't see any reason for living. All I could think was, Jenny would still be alive if I'd been a whole man, when the water hit us and knocked the wagon into kindling, instead of bein'—" He slapped his crippled leg, his whole face twisted in self-reproach.

"But Steve Benson got me through the worst of that, and took the bottle away from me and for a solid couple of weeks he never left my side, except to go find Jenny's body and put her out there on the hill alongside of our two boys. And when he pulled me through, and I told him I couldn't bear this country any longer, he named me a price for my spread and I promised him a fair chance, if he could raise it."

Burke Sully gave a short laugh. "Sounds to me like all he was doing, with his good samaritan act, was lining up something good for himself! He knows this range of yours is potentially near as valuable as Keystone itself, except it was never developed. If he can get his hands on it, I don't doubt a minute he figures he can make himself the number two kingpin, and even start crowding Troy Coldbrook!"

"That's a fact!" Wes exclaimed, drawing strength from the foreman's argument after the old man had backed him down. "And, by God, that's what I mean to prevent!"

"Now you're talking through your hats!" Abel Gannon retorted. "Steve Benson ain't that kind! He ain't even buying this for himself—he's arranging the loan and advancing the money, for all the rest of them other little outfits in that pool he belongs to. This will double their winter range, make it possible for them all to build up their beef holdings and make something worthwhile of their brands. And I'm all for 'em.

"But you, now! Troy Coldbrook ain't gonna live forever. And if the pair of you had my place, added to Keystone— and without your pa to make you head in—like as not every other outfit on the grass would find itself being crowded clear out of existence. So now you know the honest-to-God reason I won't sell to you. And I'll thank you to finish your coffee, and get the hell out of my house and off my land!"

"Not yet, damn you!" Abel Gannon had started to turn his back. In two quick strides Wes Coldbrook rounded the

36

table and his hand caught the old man's waistcoat, whirling him. "I told you this was your last chance," the young fellow said tightly, as faded blue eyes glared up at him. "Right now you're going to sit down at this table, and make me out a bill of sale!"

"The hell I am!"

The sixgun slid out of Wes Coldbrook's holster, just as Burke Sully turned from the window to exclaim, "Kid! There's somebody coming, on the town trail. Looks like it might be—"

Gannon tore loose of Wes Coldbrook and began a lunge toward the big iron stove; in alarm Coldbrook caught the gleam of a twin-barreled shotgun leaning in the corner there. But the old man's crippled leg failed him. He stumbled. Coldbrook swore and grabbed him by the collar and the sixgun rose and fell, hard. Abel Gannon went limp; his knees sagged. And young Coldbrook, with a face twisted and suffused with angry blood, struck a second time, deliberately.

It was done so quickly that Burke Sully had no time to do more than stare. He saw the old man go down to the floor like a loose sack of clothing—saw Wes Coldbrook, lowering the gun, move his shoulders as though to rid them of a binding weight.

The breath left Sully in a gusty break of sound. "What the hell have you done?" he exclaimed hoarsely.

Wes, staring at the crumpled shape on the floor in front of him, moved his lips but nothing came out. Striding over, Sully pushed him out of the way and went down to one knee. The old man's body gave limply as he rolled it over onto its back. He looked at the eyes, found them open and rolled up into the battered skull, a half-moon of white showing. He lifted his head slowly.

"Boy," he said, "I think maybe you done for him!"

V

"YOU DON'T MEAN, he's—?" The word stuck on young Coldbrook's tongue, his strangled voice failing him. He pushed Sully aside, went to his knees and fumbled frantically for a heartbeat. Sully gave him a look of withering contempt.

"What would you expect? Why'd you have to do a stupid thing like that?"

"I—I didn't mean to!" Wes stammered. "Never aimed to hit him so hard. But he was going for that shotgun. . . ." Suddenly aware of the weapon still in his own hand, he looked at it and in revulsion shoved it deep into the holster. "I don't know what got into me!"

Remembering what he had seen on the town trail, a moment ago, Burke Sully turned again to the window. Coldbrook rose hastily to join him, jarring the table with a hip in passing. The rolling swell of rangeland showed empty, under the blue dome of sky, but he could see a stain of dust hanging over the farther loops of the town trail. The riders appeared to have vanished momentarily, into a dip in the rangeland.

Coldbrook asked hoarsely, "Is it Benson?"

"And Joe Niles. That's who it looked like."

A trickle of sweat broke and rolled down the younger man's ribs. He fumbled again at the sixshooter, started to pull it up. But Burke Sully said sharply, "Leave that thing where it is! You've done enough damage."

"Burke!" Young Coldbrook had lost every shred of arrogance; he pleaded with his father's foreman, very near the edge of panic. "You got to help me!"

Not answering, Burke Sully swung about and strode to the kitchen's rear door, flung it open. After a thoughtful look outside, he turned back. "Give me a hand," he ordered.

He was already beside Gannon's motionless body, stooping to gather the limp weight into his arms. Puzzled and thoroughly scared, Wes gave no argument; he followed obediently as Sully carried the limp burden outside.

Here, along the wall of the house, sweet-smelling chunks of split pine were piled high in readiness for the cold season just ahead. Wes Coldbrook watched as the foreman deposited Abel Gannon, face down, on the ground that was thickly littered with chips. "At least," he commented heavily, "the old bastard won't be selling out, now—to Benson, or anyone else!"

The other gave him a sour look. He said impatiently, "Don't stand jawing, damn it! We only got a minute. . . ."

Already he was tearing at one of the tall stacks of stovewood; it swayed a moment, then suddenly broke and toppled in a cascade, clattering down onto Gannon's motionless figure. A second one followed it. Sully stepped back, then, brushing his hands against his jeans, and glancing at Coldbrook who stood like a man paralyzed and halfway ready to be sick.

Sully was completely cool and all efficiency. "Let's hope that covers up for your stupidity," he said brusquely. "Now let's get out of here! Move!" And he gave the other man a flat-handed blow on the shoulder, broke him loose from where he stood.

A moment later they were off at a scrambling run for the place where their horses still waited, at the corral. The hound gave them a noisy send off.

The approaching pair of riders had been aware of the hound's baying from well down the trail, but it stopped before they brought the buildings in sight. When they rode up the dog started in again, but quickly caught their scent and recognized it. He stood with his chain taut and tail beginning to wag, whining eagerly as the men pulled rein and dismounted. Joe Niles said, "What were you barking at, Duke?"

"Looks like Abel's had visitors this morning." Steve Benson pointed out the fresh horse sign by the feedlot fence.

They tied their horses and walked to the house. The hound, satisfied by a word of greeting, sat on his haunches and swept the dirt in a semicircle with strokes of a feathery tail.

The kitchen was empty. "Must be out back," Niles said, indicating the rear door that stood open. Benson walked over there and called Abel Gannon's name again, still getting no answer. He stood in the doorway a moment as he searched the yard. Suddenly he stiffened.

"Oh, my God!"

"What is it?" Joe Niles demanded, startled. Benson was already hurrying outside. His partner, following, swore as he, too, caught a first glimpse of the toppled firewood, the denimed legs of the figure half buried under it.

The two of them worked with frantic haste tossing aside the lengths of sawed pinewood. Abel Gannon lay face down, a crumpled heap. Kneeling, Benson said, "This must have just happened. Body's too warm to have been lying out here on the ground for long."

"Is he dead?"

"I don't know." He thought there were no broken bones, but he had found a couple of swellings under the thinning white hair; one of them seemed to have bled slightly.

Joe Niles picked up one of the billets of firewood, weighed it in his hand. "Hate to have these land on *me!*" he said. "They must have been stacked too high. He was getting an armload and, hampered with that gimp leg, just pulled the whole works over on top of him."

Benson didn't answer. He was gathering the old man into the house, with Niles hurrying to open the door of the bedroom for him. The old brass bed had a homemade quilt; on the chest of drawers, pictures of Abel Gannon's wife and of his two sons stared from gilt frames. The three of them lay buried on the slope east of the house. Abel Gannon had outlived them all.

Benson eased him onto the bed and straightened out his limbs. He stood frowning helplessly at the pale face, the straggling hair and waxen skin, the eyes half open, the sagging mouth.

"Sure as hell looks dead to me!" Joe Niles said in a hushed voice.

"I can't find a heartbeat." But as he reached to brush the hair back from the old man's forehead, Benson thought he saw the half-lowered eyelids flutter slightly. Galvanized, he leaned closer and caught up one of the gaunted hands, began to chafe it. "Abel! Can you hear me?"

Somewhere deep in the old man's throat there was a faint echo of a groan. Steve Benson turned on his partner. "Quick!" he ordered. "Put your saddle on a fresh horse and head for town! We got to get Doc Andrews out here—fast. And the sheriff!"

Niles was halfway across the kitchen when he stopped and turned. "Sheriff?"

The other had followed him out of the bedroom and was at the stove, opening the firebox to shove in more wood. He said, over a shoulder, "I'm not satisfied this is what it's supposed to look like. Maybe a pile of pine slabs could knock him out like that—maybe it couldn't. One thing we do know, there was someone here. You heard the dog; you saw the horse sign. And, look at this."

He pointed to the table. Two cups of coffee sat on the scrubbed oilcloth, and Joe Niles touched one with his hand. "Still warm. . . ."

Benson was stooping to pick something from the middle of the floor. He came up with it—Gannon's double-barreled shotgun, that usually stood leaning in a corner. There was no indication how it had got into the middle of the floor. "And maybe you'll notice," he said, indicating the woodbox by the stove, "that thing's already as full as he could have got it!"

Joe Niles nodded slowly, his eyes narrowing. "This is for the sheriff, all right!" he grunted. "If it's what we're thinking, who do you reckon done it? Some saddle tramp, I suppose; some grubliner—or more likely a pair of them—

41

doing him in for whatever they could find. They seen us coming and beat it, after trying to cover up the best they could."

"It could be something like that," Benson agreed, his face bleak. "I'd like to check out that horse sign my ownself, while it's fresh—but Gannon has to come first. And he can't spare both of us."

Niles pulled on his hat, firmly. "Do what you can for him. I'll get you help, as fast as hossflesh will make it!"

He ran out of the house, the door slamming after him. The dog yelped a time or two; then as the drum of his horse's hoofs sprang into being and quickly dimmed as Joe Niles spurred away on the town trail. Steve Benson went back into the bedroom.

There was a heavy comforter at the foot of the bed and he unfolded it, spread it over the unconscious Abel Gannon. He listened to the silence and felt completely useless, like a man with his hands tied. Yet he knew he had no choice but remain here, to be handy if Gannon should need him.

As he pulled up a chair closer by the bed, he felt the stiff rustle of the envelope in his pocket. After all his effort, the contents seemed of little importance, now, as he sat watching the face of this little man with the shortened leg and the twisted back, who had never known a day without pain during all the last twenty years. . . .

From behind a screen of timber, Wes Coldbrook and his foreman watched a feather of dust moving along the brown ribbon of the town trail below them, caught an occasional flash of sunlight on harness metal. Coldbrook, still shaking a little, said hoarsely, "What do you make of it, Burke?"

"He's from Gannon's," the foreman said. "And really building a smoke for town."

"Yeah, but *why?*" Wes insisted. "To get the sheriff? Do you suppose they *know?* Maybe I didn't hit the old man as hard as I thought. Maybe he ain't dead. Maybe he told

42

'em—" His voice cracked in panic. Sully gave him a hard stare.

"Make up your mind, will you? *Was* he dead, or wasn't he? You said so. I was too busy thinking how to cover up for your stupid blundering."

The young fellow waggled his head. "But he must have been! You seen how he looked. Nobody could look like that and still—"

"Then stop fussing!" Sully cut him off. "Even if they should guess it wasn't no accident, they can't pin it to us. We made it away from there without anybody seeing us. Now if you'll use your head—and follow orders—we can get you out of this."

Wes Coldbrook's shoulders fell. He ran a palm across his face, wiping sweat from cheeks that were beginning to have a rasp of beard stubble, from the last time he had shaved. "I'm listening, Burke," he mumbled, all the arrogance melted from him. "Just tell me what to do!"

The other man, looking at him askance, suppressed the look of contempt that tilted a corner of his lips. *Sure*, he thought, *I'll tell you what to do—and you'll listen, and you'll do it. Because, from now on we've got a little secret that puts you, and all the Coldbrooks, right into my hand. And no way to shake loose of it—ever!*

What he said was, "Just in case the sheriff or somebody finds our tracks and takes it into his head to follow them, we'll have to make a detour up into the rockslides and throw them off."

"All right," Wes agreed, meekly enough. "We get out of this, I think I'm going to sleep for a week!"

An hour or so ago, it had been Burke Sully who complained of fatigue and the riding they had done since midnight. Now a new purpose was in him and as he lifted the reins he said harshly, "You'll do your sleeping later! First we're going to collect a crew and move some cattle."

The young man looked at him quickly. "Move it? Where?"

"Hell! If you were your pa, I wouldn't have to tell you!

43

Across our east boundary, of course—onto old man Gannon's grass. He never had any kin. With him dead, it's open range again. And if Keystone don't move quick, somebody else may grab it first."

"Right now, let's get out of here!"

VI

It was still early when, waking from a nap in her hotel room, Ruth Faris set about preparing for the crucial next step in her mission. She found herself combating a feeling of futility, of reluctance to face the ordeal she knew lay ahead. But it had to be faced, for it was the whole purpose of her coming here.

A glance from the window, over the sunfilled street below, showed her the sun riding high, in a cloudless sky of the deep blue of the high country. The timbered ridges across the valley looked, in this sparkling air, almost near enough to touch.

She washed in the china basin and combed her hair, and then as best she could brushed the traveling dress she'd removed when she lay down on the bed in her petticoat. Even a little sleep had done something to ease the exhaustion of the long train trip, but she was left with a nagging trace of headache and an awareness that she was hungry. The gangling youth who brought the pitcher of water had also fetched warm milk from the kitchen, so the baby had had a feeding and was stirring contentedly now in his blanket. Dressed again, and as ready as she supposed she would ever be, she took the bundle and left the room, carefully closing the door.

As she walked down the dark stairway, she decided she would first have to try for something to eat in the hotel dining room, and then find some way of reaching the Coldbrook place. The manager was behind his desk. She smiled as she put down her key, saying, "Can you tell where I'd find a public livery? A place with a buggy and team to rent?"

He hesitated. "You planning to go calling on Mr. Coldbrook?"

"That's right."

George Meeks drummed nervous fingers on the desk top. "Just a minute," he said suddenly, and left her standing while he went through a gate in the counter and to a door beyond the desk. He rapped, got permission to enter. Ruth Faris heard a murmur of voices through the panel, and then the man was back. He sounded nervous as he told her, "I've saved you a trip. Mr. Coldbrook came in from the ranch, only a little while ago. He'll see you now. Go right in."

"Why, thank you!" she said. "That's very kind of you." The man nodded; he looked dubious, and his manner didn't lend her much courage. But she squared her shoulders, settling the weight of the burden in her arms as she approached the door. She went through, and pushed it shut behind her.

She stood in the hotel's office, a place smelling of wax and wood and leather. There was a big desk, a tall box safe in one corner; the windows had green half-curtains across their lower panes. A rather faded-looking woman, in a beaded black dress, sat on one end of a couch opposite the window. The man in the swivel chair behind the desk was reading through some correspondence; as he stabbed a look at her, above the silver-rimmed spectacles that seemed to sit out of place upon his leathery face with its prow of a nose, she was sure she would have known, anywhere, this must be Troy Coldbrook himself.

He was big, in every way. The fact of aging showed only in a certain sagging of his cheeks and throat, in the wide swatches of gray that ran deeply through his mass of taffy-colored hair, in the reading glasses he plainly resented but had been forced to adopt. The eyes that stared at Ruth Faris above the silver frames were as piercingly blue as any younger man's; his voice was rough and vigorous as he

45

said sharply, "Well? You have business with me, young woman?"

"Yes." She took a step forward but something in the waiting stare made her timid. And, seeing this, Troy Coldbrook scowled and rapped the desk with a ropescarred knuckle.

"You swallered your tongue or something?" he demanded, in short temper. "Here I am with a year's work to catch up on—nobody but imbeciles around any more, it looks like, to bungle all a man's enterprises when for once in his life he dares to take him a little holiday! If you can't say what's on your mind—"

"I've brought you your grandson."

Troy Coldbrook blinked once but his face showed no change of expression. "What did you say?"

"If you're Wesley Coldbrook's father," she answered, refusing to be intimidated by that blue stare, "then this is your grandson."

There was a dead stillness. The woman on the couch came slowly to her feet. At the desk the old man stiffened; a hand rose, whipped the glasses from his face and dropped them onto the pile of letters that lay before him, forgotten. "Suppose we start at the beginning," he snapped. "I've never seen you before, young woman. What's your name?"

She told him.

"And just where do you claim to have known my son?"

"I didn't say I had. This is my sister Ellen's baby; she died a few days after he was born." Ruth Faris paused. The cold blue eyes bored into her.

Troy Coldbrook prodded her with a word. "Go on! Let's hear all of it."

"Your son came to Denver a year ago this summer, with a shipping herd. I didn't meet him; but my sister did, and—fell in love with him. He told her he'd come back and marry her; but he never did. It turned out he'd even given a false name."

The old man pounced on that. "Then how'd you come to know he was my son?"

46

She hesitated, a fraction of a second. "I—managed. After my sister died, I was determined to find out who was to blame."

"And now you stand there and tell me my son fathered an illegitimate child?"

"Yes! What's more, I think he should be man enough to admit the truth and shoulder his responsibilities!"

Troy Coldbrook was on his feet—a towering figure of a man, broad shoulders straight-backed despite his age. "That's a plenty!" he thundered. He lifted a pointing finger at the girl's face. "You've said your piece; I've listened to all I'm going to. Now, I suggest you get out of here."

"I won't do it! I didn't come all this way, to have you treat me and this baby like—like—" She couldn't find a word, and suddenly she was trembling so with anger that her voice failed her.

The older woman, who had gone completely unnoticed, now asked hesitantly, "May I look at him, please?"

"Stay out of this, Ada!" the big man thundered. "Don't do anything to encourage her." But Ruth, having already guessed that this must be Wes Coldbrook's mother, turned to her deliberately and drew aside a corner of the blanket. The baby blinked at the light and tried to cram his whole fist into his mouth. Ruth saw a softness come into the woman's careworn eyes; there was a sadness, too, as she raised her glance to her husband's scowling face.

"Troy, he looks just the way Wes did!"

"Damn it, at that age they all look alike! Now, did you hear me say to stay out of this?" her husband roared. "By God, it's all the woman wants—to play on your feelings, and plant some such notion in your head!"

He turned again on the girl. "It won't work, so you might as well give up. Where did you say you came from—Denver? There'll be a train through tomorrow morning, headed back that way. You be on it!" His hand dived into his pocket, brought out a couple of gold pieces which he dropped, clattering, onto the desk between them. "This will

47

take you there—and you'd better believe it's every cent you're going to get out of me, with your little scheme, and your lies!"

Slowly Ruth Faris lifted her head, meeting his arrogant stare. She hardly trusted herself to speak, for fear her teeth should chatter—from fury, not from terror. She clutched the baby against her and she cried, "Do you really think your money will buy everything? I wouldn't touch a cent of it! I want nothing at all from you—not for myself. The less I have to do with you—*and* your son—the better it will suit me!

"But something's got to be done about *him*," she added, tightlipped, as she indicated the bundle clasped in her arms. "He's never hurt anybody; it's not his fault he's here, and he deserves a fair chance. Apparently you Coldbrooks are all alike; but I'll tell you now you haven't heard the last of this. You haven't heard the last from *me!*"

She realized she was almost shouting. Her eyes stung with tears of anger. She turned abruptly, not daring to say anything further—not even certain that her shaking knees would hold her up until she reached the door. She reached it; her hand groped for the knob. Behind her, a shocked stillness was exploded by an outburst from the old man.

"Now, you wait!"

She had the door off the latch. She flung it wide and rushed through, and saw the manager staring at her, his mouth fallen open.

Troy Coldbrook strode around his desk, seeing the last flick of the woman's skirts as she went hurrying from sight up the stairs. Furious, he turned on George Meeks and watched his face drain white as he bellowed. "You repeat a word of anything you've heard here—one word—and I promise you you'll regret it!" He started to close the door in the man's bobbing, frightened face, opened it again to say, "I want that woman out of here by traintime tomorrow. Is that understood?" The door slammed under his fist and he turned to find his wife looking at him.

48

"It was Wes's baby," she repeated quietly.

"Don't be a fool," he snapped, and turned from her steady gaze.

She said no more. At the desk, Coldbrook picked up the gold coins, stared at them, closed his fist upon them. "In our position in life, I suppose we can expect this sort of thing," he said heavily. "It's only a wonder it never happened before." He thrust the coins into his pocket, picked up his glasses and stowed them away in a leather case.

"I've read enough damn letters for one morning," he growled, plucking a widebrimmed white Stetson from a corner of the desk. "I'm going to have the rig brought around for us. Wes should be home from that jaunt he took over to Bakerville yesterday. I think I'd better be getting out to the ranch so as to warn the boy exactly what's afoot. . . ."

Minutes later, filling most of the rear seat of a democrat buggy with his wife silent beside him and a Keystone puncher whipping up the team, he heard a flurry of hoofbeats and looked back. A rider was spurring into town by one of the east-valley trails, his mount's hoofs spurting dust. Looked like that fellow Niles, one of the greasy-sackers from the northern range that had outsmarted his boy Wes, and made a deal with Abel Gannon for the Gannon ranch—property that should have been joined to Keystone.

He wondered idly what would be bringing Niles into town in such a sweat; but as the democrat's team swung him on from sight he was thinking mostly that he was certainly paying for that trip to Europe. Things were in one hell of a tangle! By God, it seemed like, at his age, a man should be able to turn over the reins to others long enough to have him a little vacation. Especially when the whole idle year, in all those queer foreign places, had turned out to be nothing much but a Goddamned bore. . . .

For two spreads that had been established at nearly the same time, and under nearly the same circumstances, the contrast between Keystone and Abel Gannon's grubby home

49

quarters was considerable. It was the difference between a ranch that had taken a remarkably able man's full attention, over a score of years, and another one belonging to a cripple to whom the years had not been kind ones.

Coldbrook's main house was a solid, two-story log structure with a pair of fieldstone chimneys flanking its width, and a roofed gallery along the front. Behind it, on lower ground, stood the big barn in fresh red paint, the bunkhouse and kitchen and the smaller house where the foreman lived; and sheds, corrals, a stock pond kept full by the spring that welled up in the stone spring house. Feed lots lay beyond, filled with stacks of winter hay piled high behind barbed wire barriers. Tall poplars lined three sides of the house, spilling a rain of golden leaves into the autumn wind as Wes and Burke Sully rode in, at midday.

A spread that hired as large a crew as Keystone's usually had one or two hands around the home buildings at nearly any time, busy with some chore or other. Today a pair of riders were up on the barn roof, laying on a new patch of shakes against the winter snows ahead. Sully called them down, ordered them to get ready to ride; Wes added, "And while you're at it, one of you put my saddle on a fresh bronc. This bay's favoring its right foreleg, like it might be starting to go lame."

Vic Gilmore, the puncher who came to take the horse, looked closely and exclaimed, "Hey! The fetlock's got a long cut. Been sliced open on a sharp rock, looks like."

"Put some grease on it, then," Wes said indifferently, not bothering to examine the leg; to him a horse was something to ride, and there were always plenty others in the Keystone corrals if one happened to put itself out of commission or had to be destroyed. The bay, he supposed, had picked up that cut while he and Sully were up in the rough country losing their sign, on leaving Gannon's.

Turning, he saw Troy Coldbrook walking toward him from the direction of the house.

Wes had always looked on his father with mingled feelings of affection, resentment, and respect. The shadow of such a giant was a hard place for any fellow to grow up, constantly measuring himself and aware of the poor showing he made by comparison—burning with the constant need of somehow earning the old man's respect or even, if possible, outstripping his achievements. Just now Wes could tell he was riled about something and he quelled a start of alarm—the reaction he always had, of wondering: *What has he found out about me? Could he possibly know about the train robbery, or—God forbid!—the death of Abel Gannon?*

He waited, as Troy Coldbrook strode solidly toward him with the sun striking full against his blocky face, his graying beard bared to the crisp wind. The old man halted, shoved his thumbs behind his belt and said, "So, you got back. Any luck at Bakerville?"

Wes had been vague about the supposed business trip he'd invented to cover his absence last night, and he was vague now in answering. "Didn't pan out. The stock he had to sell didn't look like much." His father merely wagged his head. Wes found himself relaxing a trifle. Whatever was on his father's mind, it could hardly be either one of the dreaded possibilities that had so filled him with alarm.

The old man said, "Something's come up. Ain't too important but it is a kind of damned nuisance. Maybe we better go to the house and talk it over."

Before Wes could answer, there was an interruption as Burke Sully rode up and, holding in his restless mount, nodded to the older man as he told Wes, "We're ready to trail when you are."

Troy appeared to catch a hint of something urgent here. He looked quickly from one to the other and said, "What's going on?"

He would have to have an answer. Wes drew a long breath. "Guess you hadn't heard, Pa. It's Abel Gannon."

"What about him?"

"He's dead. We heard it in town," he went on, improvising hastily. "Something about his woodpile collapsing on top of him."

"The hell you say!" The bushy brows drew down above unfaded blue eyes; a stern look of shock dug deep grooves into Troy's cheeks, drew his mouth out long and hard. Troy Coldbrook swore, slowly and forcefully; it was his way of expressing grief. He shook his head then and said, in a hard voice, "Well—at least now he won't be selling his property. Not to Steve Benson—not even to *you*."

There was a bitter irony in his voice as he said this, and it whipped a sudden stain into his son's face. Troy had had many caustic things to say, on returning home from Europe and learning the circumstances of the deal by which Benson had got the inside track with old Gannon. He seemed to blame the whole situation on some failing of Wes, himself.

Stung, the young man hit back in his own defense. "I'm takin' care of Benson," he said stoutly. "That's where I'm on my way to, now—to move a herd across onto Horseshoe Meadow, and hold it for Keystone before him or some of them other greasy-sackers get the notion. I figure it's open range again," he pointed out, carefully not looking at Burke Sully—avoiding the foreman's expression as he quoted Sully's words as though they were his own. "It'll be first come, first served. I figure to take what I want and not have to pay even a cent for it. . . ."

He stopped, seeing the new look on his father's face. The big head had lifted, the hatchet of a nose was widened at the nostrils like that of an animal catching a good scent. "It will take more men than you got here," Troy Coldbrook declared flatly. He turned to Burke Sully, then, giving out orders—and already Wes knew that he, in his turn, had been shoved aside. The reins were being lifted from his hands as his father assumed command, exactly as though the plan had been his own to begin with.

Even being away a year, Troy seemed to know everything about Keystone—where the herds were spotted, what each man was doing. Within a matter of minutes, one puncher was being sent as a courier to fetch the extra riders he needed, with the orders that would start Keystone beef moving toward what had been the boundary with Abel Gannon's grass. Another was hurrying to rope out a horse and pile old Coldbrook's saddle on it, while Troy and Sully conferred hastily on strategy.

And left to one side, forgotten, Wes Coldbrook could only grit his teeth in angry frustration.

VII

IT SEEMED THAT Joe Niles had been gone hardly any time at all, when Benson started measuring the time before he could be expected to return with the doctor in tow. With a fresh horse from Gannon's corral under him, Niles was bound to make good time reaching town; an hour, perhaps, should see him there. Then it would depend on his success in locating Seth Andrews and in the doctor's being free to return with him promptly. Andrews wasn't young. With the best intentions in the world, there were limits to how fast he could travel.

Benson had stolen a few moments to unsaddle his horse, and turn it into the corral. After that, he didn't allow himself to wander from the old man's bedside. Since Gannon still felt cold, he kept up the fire even though the house was already stifling. He helped himself to some of the stew he found simmering on the back of the stove. A dozen times he found himself at the window, watching the town trail, always finding it empty.

At last, with nothing useful to do with his time, he filled a coffee cup and carried it into the bedroom where he set it on a corner of the dresser in easy reach of his chair. He checked Abel Gannon's condition, found him unchanged— sunken face ashen-colored against the pillow, thinning hair askew, breathing shallow and irregular. More than once Benson's own breath had clogged in his throat at hearing

53

that laboring sound break off, only to resume again with a sudden drag of air that rushed to fill the old man's lungs. It was an anxious, nerve-wracking vigil.

Seated in the stream of sunlight through the bedroom window, he became aware of a certain heaviness of his senses. It was the monotony of waiting, the warmth of the room, the steady tick of a cheap alarm clock on the dresser—all this, together with his poor success at sleeping on the train, the night before. Though he fought to stay awake, even anxiety, and the coffee he had been drinking, seemed little help.

Suddenly his head lifted with a neck-popping jerk. At first he was aware only that the square of sunlight lying on the floor had shifted; then he heard the nearing sound of a pair of horses. A moment later the hound, on his tether in the yard, sent up a hollow bugling. Benson got quickly to his feet and went through the kitchen, stepping outside as Rufe Waller and Sam Tremaine pulled up before the house and dismounted.

These were his neighbors who, together with still another rancher named Harry York, made up the balance of the Pool that was interested in the purchase of Abel Gannon's range. They were older men than Benson—men with wives and kids, gone gray in the hard struggle of trying to build something like security for their families. Steve Benson, who had no responsibility to anyone but himself and his partner, felt a very honest humility at the comparison. These, he thought, were the real conquerors—the true heroes. As he'd told Laurel Whitney, a big part of his satisfaction in the deal with Abel Gannon had been knowing it would give his friends the basis for a more promising future.

Now, all that was left in doubt. The two had anxious looks on them. In answer to Benson's question Rufe Waller —a stocky, gray-haired man who had seen so many tough breaks that they gave him a tendency to pessimism—explained their presence here: "I ran into Joe Niles heading for town, and he told me what happened. I figured I better spread the word. I rode and got Sam, and he sent his boy

54

over to Harry's place. Reckon he should be along pretty soon."

"How's Gannon making it?" Sam Tremaine demanded.

"I just don't know," Benson admitted. "He's breathing, but far as I can see that's about all."

"Let's have a look."

They tramped inside and stood silently regarding the motionless figure in the bed. Rufe Waller, the pessimist, shook his head and said somberly, "Ain't this a hell of a thing to happen to any man? And aside from that, supposing he don't come out of it—supposing he should die. What happens to our deal?"

"*You* figure it out," Benson said bleakly. Sam Tremaine rubbed a lantern jaw, mild brown eyes frowning unhappily behind steelframed spectacles. "Joe Niles said you brought the money back from Denver with you, too! Just a couple of signatures on a piece of paper, and we'd have been all fixed up." He added, after a moment, "Poor old guy! Joe said something about the woodpile falling over on him."

"Come on in the kitchen," Benson suggested. "I'll tell you as much as we know."

The pair shucked their windbreakers, against the stuffy heat of the place, and Benson poured coffee for them. He didn't know how long they had been seated at the plank table, discussing this turn of events, when a sound of hoofs and wheels and a renewed outburst from the dog brought them to their feet. Doc Andrews was just pulling a rig to a halt outside. He was alone.

Sam Tremaine went to hold the heads of the team for him as the doctor got stiffly down. Seth Andrews was getting a little old for long rides like this one; Steve Benson stepped in quickly and steadied him as he worked the stiffness out of cramped knee joints. "Where's Joe?" Benson demanded.

"Said something about looking for the sheriff," Andrews said as he reached to get his bag. "I understand Tom Faw-

55

cett went out to check on that trouble at Dead Man, last night—don't know if he's back yet."

While the other two took care of the team, Benson and the doctor went inside. Andrews was quite at home here; he had known Abel Gannon for years, had made the trip often to take care of that crippled leg. He had twice delivered sons to Abel and his wife, and seen them both dead and buried on the hill overlooking the ranch yard. Now, as he walked into the bedroom and set his black bag on the dresser where he had placed it so many times before, he shook his head, clucking his tongue, and muttered, "It's a sad house, Benson—a damned sad house!"

He turned to his patient, leaned and thumbed the eyelids open, his lips pursed. Then, looking around, he saw the other man watching silently at the foot of the bed. "Look! Why don't you go join your friends and let me make my examination in peace? Anything you can do, I'll tell you quick enough."

"All right," Steve Benson said, and went out closing the door behind him.

He and Rufe Waller and Sam Tremaine were seated in heavy silence about the kitchen table when the old doctor finally emerged, rolling down his shirtsleeves. They waited in tense expectation but Andrews seemed unconscious of their unspoken questions; instead he deliberately buttoned his sleeves, dropped the coat he was carrying over the back of a chair, and turned to the stove. He got a cup from the shelf, filled it from the coffeepot, and brought it to the table. He took his seat and, breathing asthmatically, busied himself with shoveling two heaping spoons of sugar into the cup and lacing it with canned milk.

Finally Tremaine could stand it no longer. "Well?" he demanded.

The doctor gave him a reproachful look and deliberately tried a sip of the coffee, smacking his lips over it. He set the cup down before he would answer.

"Abel Gannon's a sick man," he pronounced; it was no

56

more than they already knew for themselves. "Knock on the head like he took, I've seen people that come out of it—and again, I've seen 'em lie for days and die without once stirring or making a sign. He might pull through, and again he might not. Abel ain't too strong, you know." He took another drag at the coffee; his aging hand trembled a little, holding the cup.

He might be an old man, almost feeble himself; but Steve Benson knew he was still thoroughly capable, with a mind as sharp as it had ever been. He asked the doctor, "Do you think it's a skull fracture?"

"Little hard to say; hate to put enough pressure on the bone to find out for certain. He took two bad ones, right to the base of the skull, maybe an inch apart. One broke the skin. In addition, he's got some nasty bruises in the region of his back and shoulders."

Rufe Waller put in quickly, "That'd be when the woodpile fell on him."

Andrews looked at him with eyes that revealed nothing. "Yeah," the old doctor said finally. "That'd be when he got the bruises, I reckon." The way he said it made Benson look at him sharply.

"Sounds like you're hinting that's not how he got hit on the head."

The faded eyes looked at him blandly, then turned to consider the woodbox by the stove. "Well, now," Andrews said in his quiet voice, "that pine is pretty light stuff, to hurt anybody that much just from falling over on him. . . ."

The same thought had been in Steve Benson's mind, but he let it go without comment.

The hound began sounding off again and Sam Tremaine, at the window, said, "Here's Harry York—and he's coming hell for leather. I wonder what that boy of mine told him!" Harry York was a big man, with a big man's deliberate pace of movement; but there was nothing slow-paced about the way he came tearing into the Gannon yard, lifting powder dust as he scooped out a hurried turn and a halt

57

before the doorway. The yellow dust thinned and the coat of his blue roan gelding showed darkly shining with sweat.

The other Pool ranchers came filing out to greet him, leaving Doc Andrews incuriously enjoying his second cup of coffee at the kitchen table. York lowered his weight stolidly from the saddle; Steve Benson, moving out to catch the roan's headstall and help to settle him, said, "You didn't have to hurry this much. There's nothing any of us can do here. Gannon's unconscious and the doc says we just have to wait and see if, and how soon, he pulls out of it."

Harry York swabbed dirt and sweat from his broad cheeks with a wide palm. "It's a hell of a note; sure enough," he agreed darkly. "But that ain't why I was burning leather just now."

"Why then?" Benson snapped, catching something in his manner. "You got news of your own, it looks like."

"Well, it was news to me—and it don't look like good news. There's a big dust building over in the direction of Horseshoe Meadow; Sam's boy found me over on West Creek, and I seen it from there. I'd say it's cattle moving— a sizable bunch of cattle."

The others exchanged a look. "Cattle?" Rufe Waller echoed, blankly; and Sam Tremaine added, "I don't see how that could be! Abel Gannon's got no beef in that section. He's got hardly enough stock left, altogether, to make a dust of any size."

"We're all thinking the same, I guess," Steve Benson said slowly.

"If there's cattle moving in the vicinity of Horseshoe," Harry York said flatly, "I'm thinking there's only one place it could be moving from. That grass is just this side of the boundary with Keystone. And Coldbrook beef sure as hell has no business being there!"

"There doesn't seem to be any other answer," Benson agreed, nodding. "Yet, the Coldbrooks have never violated that boundary, in all the years they've been neighbors with Gannon—not even since he fell on bad times, and thinned

58

out his herds so that he wasn't using much of it. Troy Cold-brook can be pretty damned ruthless sometimes, when it suits him; but somehow this just don't sound like Troy."

"It could be Wes," Rufe Waller suggested darkly. "Or Burke Sully."

Benson nodded again. "I kind of think," he said in an edged voice, "we ought to take a look. Long as Doc's in charge there's damn little more for the rest of us to do here; and with Gannon flat on his back, somebody has to look after his interests. Anyway, it's our concern too, if Keystone is suddenly trying a land-grab!"

They were all instantly agreed. Within minutes the four were mounted and cutting out of the yard. Doc Andrews, in the doorway, stood and watched them go.

VIII

STEVE BENSON FOUND it an actual relief to be moving, to be enjoying physical activity again after his vigil at Gannon's bedside. Even if it meant danger, this was a kind of danger he understood. He would almost rather face a cocked gun than the eerie silence of that house, the rasping, shaky tremble of that struggling effort to breathe.

Here in the mountains, at this season of the year, dusk came early. The four Pool members pushed their mounts hard; the low sun hung directly in their faces, and the pine-fresh wind that pressed back low-pulled hatbrims already contained a chill hint of the coming evening.

A long hogback ridge, with timber reaching in tongues of pine and aspen up the broken face that overlooked Horse-shoe Meadow, offered a vantage point where they could see what was happening. They pulled in their blowing horses. An expanse of brown-cured grass stretched below them—rich grass, one of the prizes of this range. Here, cattle brought down from summer range could put on the money-fat that told all the difference, once they were moved to market.

But today cattle were pouring onto Horseshoe that had no business being there—close to two hundred head of white-faces, Benson judged, making rapid saddle-count. Squinting against the sunsmear in the west, he tried to identify the half dozen riders that moved at the periphery of the meadow, where the skirt of timber down the flanking ridges thinned; but the distance was too great.

Saddle leather popped as Rufe Waller shifted position. "Well," he said heavily, "what do you make of it?"

Benson didn't answer. A trio of horsemen had just moved out of a clump of willows that edged a meandering stream, on the nearer side of the herd. These were close enough that the golden light, casting shadows long across the meadow bottom, made recognition of them easy. "Troy Coldbrook!" Harry York exclaimed. "And Wes—and Burke Sully! By God, now we know!"

Benson drew a breath. "I still can't imagine Troy Coldbrook doing anything as highhanded as moving in on a neighbor's grass, without permission."

"Maybe," Sam Tremaine suggested, "he *had* permission. Maybe Abel Gannon changed his mind, while you were in Denver. For all any of us know, Gannon could of got tired waiting for his money, and decided to close a deal with Keystone instead."

"After all," Rufe Waller pointed out, "Troy Coldbrook was his neighbor, a long time before the rest of us."

"It's possible, of course," Benson admitted. "But it don't sound like a thing Gannon would do—not without letting us know."

"Then it sure as hell looks as though Coldbrook has got some explaining to do!"

Steve Benson lifted the reins. "So let's ride on down there and see if he's of a mind to explain to us. . . ."

They dropped down the slope in single file, picking their way, moving from golden light into gathering shadow. The Meadow was a bowl swimming with early dusk; as they descended, the sun went down from sight behind yonder ridge and Steve Benson found his eyes almost ached with relief to have its glare taken away from them.

The three Keystone men were deep in talk and failed to notice the approaching riders. But now Troy Coldbrook's head lifted and he visibly stiffened. At once a word from him brought Wes and Burke Sully twisting about in the saddle; to a jerk of the reins and kick of bootheels, they swung their horses around. Coldbrook and his son and foreman sat and watched the newcomers.

When they had covered perhaps half the distance Burke Sully, suddenly and without warning, slipped his saddle carbine and laid it across his knees. Steve Benson heard a grunt of alarm break from Sam Tremaine. At the same moment Wes Coldbrook, as though taking his cue from Sully, dragged his own rifle free. Benson's jaw firmed but he told his companions, "Easy! Let's not get excited!"

Under his breath, Harry York exclaimed, "Excited? Hell! Them things can *kill* you!"

All four had halted, almost without thinking. Now Benson pressed a heel to his mount's flank, sending it forward again. It had taken only a couple of steps when Burke Sully yelled something and whipped the carbine to his shoulder. White smoke tipped its muzzle. Rifle lead stamped into the ground several yards ahead of Benson, raising a quick geyser of dirt. A split second later the rifle's report slapped out across the sounds of the milling herd, and ran in rolling echoes along the hills that cupped the meadow.

Harry York lifted an angry shout: "Hey, damn it!"

For answer, both Sully and Wes Coldbrook fired and worked their rifle levers and fired again. An angry-sounding slug split the air between Steve Benson and Sam Tremaine, making the latter duck his head between his shoulders. Harry York jerked out a sixgun but Benson told him, "No!" Really angry, and alarmed, Benson stood in the stirrups and whipping off his hat swung it above his head, in a wigwag signal. He sent a yell across the distance: "Troy! Troy Coldbrook! Will you talk to us?"

No reply from the elder Coldbrook who sat unmoving, showing no sign of having even heard him; instead the saddle guns in the hands of Sully and Wes Coldbrook lashed out again. Up to now the shots had seemed meant to warn them back, but this time a steel-jacketed slug dug into the dirt close enough to spatter Rufe Waller's horse with bits of shattered stone, stinging the animal and setting it dancing out of control. Troy Coldbrook meanwhile had brought his own saddle gun into the open, though not yet to his shoulder. But Sam Tremaine had had enough.

"Let's get out of here!" he yelled. "Damn it, they mean business!"

With more Keystone riders spurring up from the direction of the herd, quick retreat seemed the only sensible move. Benson led it, thinking only of the useless waste and sacrifice for their families if any of these men with him should stop a bullet. The shooting quit off, on the instant that they yanked their horses around and kicked them up the slope of the ridge; but he kept going until they were into the protection of a scatter of pine halfway up its face. Here they pulled rein and looked apprehensively at one another. "That could have been nasty!" Harry York exclaimed on a gust of breath.

Rufe Waller had slipped from the saddle to look at his horse. Fragments of rock had stung it but done no real damage. Calming the frightened animal, Rufe said, "Only one thing makes any sense. Our first guess was right: They're taking over by force!"

"But Troy Coldbrook should know he can't get away with it," Sam Tremaine insisted. "There's still law in this country!"

"Yeah? What do you think the sheriff will have to say about *this?*"

Harry York was darkly skeptical. "Tom Fawcett ain't tough enough to buck Keystone! I say the time to stop this thing is right now. And we're the ones to do it."

Rufe shook his head, unhappy with the way things were going. He appealed to Benson. "What do you say, Steve?"

Steve Benson had been keeping his own counsel through this, because he was bothered by certain troubling thoughts of his own. Two men, he reminded himself, had boarded the train at Dead Man and tried to lift the money which was meant to pay Abel Gannon for his property; later, two men had stopped at Gannon's place and now Gannon lay close to death, knocked down by what might or what might not have been an accident. This seemed to add up to something. At the least it was an ugly set of coincidences, and the more he thought it over the less he liked it.

He said slowly, "I'm inclined to agree with Harry. I'm not in a mood to give up this easy. I still want to talk to Troy Coldbrook—even if I have to sneak up and throw a gun on him and make him listen. Just maybe, though, if I was to go back down there alone—"

Harry York protested. "Not alone, Steve! It ain't worth the risk!"

Sam Tremaine was in quick agreement. "Hell, we couldn't even give you any kind of decent support! Not at this distance—hand guns against saddle rifles."

"At least," Harry York insisted, "you got to let me go with you. You can do the talking, if there is any. But I'm. gonna be there, to cover your back."

Benson considered and gave in. "All right," he said. "Rufe, you and Sam stay here and keep out of the way. Harry and I will go down." Harry had his impulsive side and Benson hoped he would be able to keep the big man from doing anything foolish.

The entire slope was in shadow, now, and night would be gathering on the Meadow before too much longer. Benson pointed to a shallow draw, choked with brush and aspen, that looked as though it offered shelter for most of the distance to the base of the hogback. "That way," he said and led out. A slight bulge in the face of the slope gave them some protection from below, until they had gained the head of the draw, itself. Once into this, the going was quicker and they made their way down its steep course, with the white-boled aspen raining golden leaves on them.

Benson found himself listening for danger signals, but could hear nothing above the noise of their own horses breaking through brush and rattling loose stones that floored the draw. The fact that the rifles had quit seemed to indicate the Keystone men were satisfied they'd been driven off. Now the draw began to level off. At its brushchoked mouth, Benson pulled up to make a hurried check.

The first thing he saw, not fifty yards away, was Troy Coldbrook himself—dismounted and standing with one hand on the saddlehorn and the other holding his rifle by the breech, as he peered up at the face of the hill; plainly he was still bothered, still expecting renewed trouble from there. A little farther on were two of the Keystone riders, and Wes Coldbrook talking to another one. There was no sign at all of Burke Sully.

Troy turned now, thrust his long gun into the saddle scabbard and bent to turn the stirrup for his boot. Steve Benson told his companion, "Stay back and cover me." He kicked his mount and broke out of the brush, making directly toward the rancher.

Coldbrook lifted into the saddle, with all the natural ease of his breed. He apparently hadn't yet glimpsed the rider making toward him. A yank at the reins started his big horse back in the direction of the herd. And Steve Benson lifted his voice in a shout: "Hold it there, Troy!" Grimly he fed the spurs to his mount and stretched him out into an all-out run, determined to close the distance.

When the rifle shot came he never knew from what direction. He felt it strike the barrel of the horse between his knees and had that much warning—that much time to kick free of the stirrups. Next moment the horse started to go down in a somersaulting fall, and he launched himself from the saddle and went limp with a rider's training. He struck the ground on hip and shoulder; earth and sky wheeled about him as he rolled.

64

Motionless and stunned, while the world settled its spinning, he lay and heard a swelling of gunfire, and a tremble of pounding hoofs carried to him through the ground. The Meadow and the hillside seemed to be erupting; with an effort of will he rolled and pulled himself onto hands and knees and then to a kneeling position. The body of the dead horse, close by, cut off some of his view but he saw Keystone riders firing at the timber where Sam Tremaine and Rufe Waller had holed up and were working their hand guns—trying, Benson thought, to divert his enemies' attention.

Still dazed, he turned his head then; and there was Wes Coldbrook spurring toward him, rifle in his grasp. Wes had a wild and reckless look, that startled Benson into action. He stumbled to his feet, reaching for holster. Wes fired. Lead struck soddenly into a half-rotted windfall, as Benson's fingers closed on emptiness: The gun had been jarred loose, in his fall. Wes was still coming, working the rifle lever to jack out the spent shell. Benson looked around, frantically searching for his own weapon. And it was then that he heard Harry York's shout: "Steve! This way!"

Harry was coming to the rescue, shoe irons spattering Benson with grit as the horse plowed to a tricky, turning halt there on the slope of the hill. Putting himself and his mount as a shield between Benson and Wes Coldbrook, Harry York twisted about and fired at an angle across his own body. Though he missed, his shot came close enough to startle Wes and make him slow his pellmell rush; satisfied with that for the moment, Harry leaned and offered his arm for Steve Benson to catch. A lift helped Benson spring to a place behind the saddle. As he settled there, Harry yelled at the horse and roweled it upslope again, toward the draw and the protection of the aspens.

Looking back, Benson saw Wes Coldbrook holding his bronc on a rough rein while he emptied his rifle's magazine after them, every shot going wild in his hurried excitement. Three other Coldbrook riders were coming at a run, trying

65

to cut them off. But then the horse crashed through brush at the mouth of the draw and as the trees closed around them Harry York pulled quickly broadside, to fling a couple of bullets at the approaching riders and make them rein in quickly.

"By God!" he said through clenched teeth. "We'll show 'em now! They just try to knock us out of here—"

"No! Keep going," Steve Benson ordered; and as the other twisted an astonished look at him: "We can't hold them off —not with just one gun. I've lost mine!"

The big fellow cursed as he saw it was true; he swung his shoulders angrily but, twisting around again, stabbed his gun into holster and kicked with the spurs. The bronc plunged ahead, up through the draw where dusk was gathering by the moment.

Benson had trouble holding to his place behind the saddle. The pursuit appeared to have ended, for the moment at least—apparently those Keystone men had no taste for following them in here. Above the scrabbling of the horse's hoofs and the crash of brush and branches, Benson thought he heard an occasional gunshot, supposed that Waller and Tremaine were still trying to keep Keystone occupied.

They reached a tongue of rubble, and had to fight their way across this in an open space where the trees fell back temporarily. They had nearly crossed it, and Benson was about to slip from his place in order to help the struggling mount when he saw Harry York give a lurch and knew he had been hit. Harry caught at the horn, but he was already slumping sideward as Benson managed to take his stocky weight. It was all Benson could do to break his fall and, dismounting, ease the hurt man to the ground. The riderless horse scrambled on a little farther before it lagged to a halt in the tangle of growth.

Everything else was forgotten when he saw the bloodless pallor of bullet shock in his friend's face. Harry York had the biggest heart in the world. He also had a wife and three kids at home on that hard-scrabble ranch of his. Trembling a little, Steve Benson got his back against a boulder. Harry was breathing shallowly, as blood began to leak and spread a red stain on the shoulder of his blanket coat. But when Benson tried to unfasten the coat and pull it open, the hurt man groaned and with a shake of his head fought to jerk free. "No!"

"Harry! I got to take a look at it!"

"Leave me be!" the other exclaimed, rocking his shoulders against the boulder in a paroxysm of pain. "Leave me be! I'm scared to look!"

"Maybe it's not as bad as you think. We have to get it tied up enough to stop the bleeding, so we can get out of here fast!" Otherwise, Benson was thinking, their best hope was that Coldbrook's men would hold off until solid darkness came. He didn't know whether they had that long, because he was at a loss to understand Coldbrook's intentions. But he did know that this was no spot for a stand; brush and trees hampered his view, and prevented him from learning what Keystone might be up to.

He pulled Harry's hand away from the wound, and this time the hurt man let him have his way. Benson got the coat open and managed to pull the shirt down off York's shoulder. He grunted at what he saw, but there was relief in his voice as he said, "It don't really look too bad. The bullet went clean through the muscle, doesn't appear to have touched the bone."

Harry took courage to risk a look, and gave a shuddering sigh as he decided Benson had assessed the damage correctly. Steve Benson dug into a pocket for his handkerchief, to make a bandage. He was like that, off balance, when a sound above and behind him brought his head quickly around. He froze then, seeing the man silhouetted on the edge of the gully, and the rifle leveled in his hands.

IX

Burke Sully's face was in shadow, but his whole frame seemed to exude a smug triumph. "Got you now, Benson," he said heavily. "I got you good!"

"Looks like it," Benson admitted. His own gun was lost and Harry York's was in his holster, out of reach.

"Wasn't for not trying that I didn't get you before. First try, I dropped your horse. Second time, looks like your friend took it instead. Well, I don't see how I can miss again!" The carbine came to a rest, centered squarely on Steve Benson's chest; he felt his breath catch in his throat as though it had solidified there.

Until that encounter in the train coach at Dead Man Summit, he had never given much thought to Burke Sully except as an unapproachable, hard-tempered man who was an exacting foreman. Benson had certainly never suspected such depths of rancor and hatred in him. Or—he wondered suddenly—was it really ambition, and the thwarting of his will in last night's holdup attempt, that spoke now in the foreman's angry voice?

Something gave him the reckless daring to say, "If you'd had enough sleep last night, maybe you'd be shooting a little straighter!"

A stillness came between them; into it, Burke Sully said, in a harsh voice, "I dunno what you're talking about!"

"Don't you?" Having said that, Benson decided he'd said enough. To continue taunting the man was foolish risk, with a rifle in his hands and Sully in an uncertain mood.

That the Keystone foreman understood well enough what he'd been hinting, seemed plain enough from the next words, spoken in a tight and breathy whisper: "By God! Maybe you don't realize I could plug the both of you—right where you sit—and claim it was self-defense! Nobody'd ever ask me any questions."

"Oh, yes they would," Benson retorted quickly. "Happens we've only got one gun, between us. You'd have hard going to make self-defense out of *that!*" He added, "Besides, it sounds like you've just run out of time. . . ."

Even as he spoke, the sounds of several riders came plainer through the dusk. Steve Benson had been half-consciously aware that the firing—from the pines, and from the floor of the Meadow—had thinned and stopped. Now, in the returned evening stillness, saddle leather creaked and hoofs sluffed the rubble of the hillside. Troy Coldbrook's voice came across the fading light: "Burke! Burke Sully! Sing out—where the hell are you?"

The foreman's head jerked around as he heard his name. He whipped a glance again toward his prisoners, and the carbine lifted in his hands as though he were furiously debating whether to go ahead and use it. The near approach of the horsemen, and another call from his boss, must have decided him—he had no time, now, and with a muttered curse he lowered the carbine. "Here!" he shouted answer, and brought the riders quickly toward them.

Benson filled his lungs as the scared tightness left them; he could only guess at the outcome, if it hadn't been for this interruption. But now the horsemen came on at a canter, to form a milling clot at the edge of the gully; besides Troy Coldbrook and Wes, he recognized Sheriff Fawcett and his own partner, Joe Niles. He had never seen a more welcome pair of men.

It was Niles who cried anxiously. "That you, Steve? You okay? Who's down there with you?"

"Harry York. He's taken a slug through his arm," Benson answered crisply. "It should be all right, once I can get it bound up and stop the bleeding."

"Who did it to him? Sully? By God, if—"

The foreman growled a retort, and then Troy Coldbrook shut them both up. It would seem to be Sheriff Fawcett's role to take charge here, being the one with legal jurisdiction; but the rancher was not one to pass the reins to anyone. He told Burke Sully, "Go get your horse—and put up that damned carbine. That's an order! Benson, I want to talk to you."

"I been trying to talk to *you*," the latter retorted angrily. "But you and your men seem to be more for shooting first, and talking later. Now, you can damn well wait until I've done what I can for Harry York!"

He turned back to the job Burke Sully had interrupted, letting Coldbrook stew. Using his handkerchief he tied up the wound that appeared to have stopped its worst bleeding. He pulled the coat back up over the bandage, and rose, saying, "That'll do for now. Just take it easy a minute, Harry. We'll get you on your horse and take you to Gannon's, and the doc can finish it." Leaving him, he turned and went scrambling up out of the draw to confront the Keystone boss.

The newcomers had dismounted, and now Burke Sully came walking back leading his horse and looking dangerously sullen. There was still sufficient grainy light to make out faces. Troy Coldbrook's arrogant stare held anger and puzzlement. "Benson," he said gruffly, "looks like there might have been a mistake made, here. Sheriff just came from Abel Gannon's place, with Niles. They tell me Abel's not dead."

"Did you have any reason to think he might be?"

"I was told so." The old rancher turned on his son, then, to demand, "Wes! Just where did you hear that, anyway?"

The younger Coldbrook seemed paralyzed. With all their eyes staring at him, in the grainy twilight, he made an apparent effort to speak. "Well, I—I heard," he faltered. His glance roamed aimlessly, but when it touched Burke Sully's face he suddenly seemed to find confidence. He turned back to his father to explain, in a stronger voice, "I mean, I got it from Burke."

Steve Benson thought he saw the foreman's head jerk sharply. Troy scowled. "Oh?"

"That's right." Warming to his story, Wes spilled it out. "On the way in, this morning, he left me at the forks while

70

he made a side trip into town for something. Later he caught up with me on the road—said someone told him Joe Niles had been in looking for the sheriff, and that Abel Gannon was dead."

Troy Coldbrook swore, and swung his piercing stare at his foreman. "Next time, get your facts straight—hear? You see what you've gone and made me do!" Not waiting or giving Sully a chance to reply, he turned to the sheriff. "Well, you've heard the story. Abel was reported dead, and I knew he had no heirs. That meant his spread would revert to open range, and I figured to claim what I needed of it before someone else got in ahead of me and cut me out. So, I moved this herd onto the Horseshoe."

"Now maybe you see what *we* were up to," Steve Benson finished. "Looked to us Keystone was moving in on a neighbor's range. Gannon's not dead, but he's bad hurt and unable to protect his own grass. We figured we should try to do it for him."

"Hell!" Troy Coldbrook exploded, really angry—and, probably, cruelly humiliated over the way things had turned out. "You ought to know me better than that! Why, Abel Gannon's been my friend and neighbor, for twenty years and longer! I tell you, it was an honest mistake!"

The sheriff put in his word, then. "I'm sure it couldn't have been anything else, Troy. I was sure of it when Doc Andrews told us about these men having seen dust of a herd being moved, and riding out to investigate. I knew there had to be some good explanation."

"In that case," Benson said coldly, "naturally he won't have any objection to pulling this herd of his back across Keystone boundary where it's supposed to be."

"And naturally," Joe Niles put in quickly, "he's gonna want to replace Steve Benson's horse, that was shot from under him."

Troy Coldbrook's anger fairly crackled, as he swung his head like a baited and angry bull. "You're all going a little fast!" he exclaimed. "Before I do a single thing, I want to

71

see Abel Gannon for myself. I'm heading for his place right now. I aim to find out exactly what the hell's going on here. . . ."

The old cattleman spent a long five minutes alone in the bedroom where Abel Gannon lay unconscious; when he came out into the kitchen his face looked drawn and tired and he moved with a wooden stiffness. He ran his stare over the faces of the men gathered there, turned to Doc Andrews who was working to bind up Harry York's hurt arm while Steve Benson held a lamp.

Coldbrook said gruffly, "I want you to do your best for that man in there, Doc. I was in Europe when his bad trouble hit him last spring; I didn't know, and so I couldn't help him. But this time, I want him to have the best of care—you understand?"

Doc Andrews nodded, not pausing with the work his hands were doing. "I'm planning to spend the night here with him. Come morning, if it looks safe, I'll take him in to my place in town."

The rancher nodded curt satisfaction. "If you need help taking care of him, then get it. Get anything at all. And send me the bill."

He looked around the room. The kitchen held a certain tension, with the Coldbrooks and Burke Sully facing the members of the Pool. Troy Coldbrook's glance touched on the man his foreman had shot, and hastily slid on. He never was one to make apologies for mistakes, and he offered none now. All he would say, grudgingly, was, "I'll have my boys move that herd off Horseshoe Meadow tomorrow, first thing."

At that the sheriff, leaning his hips against the edge of the table with a coffee cup in his hand, showed a look of plain relief. "I told you, boys," he said triumphantly, looking at Joe Niles, "that this was all a misunderstanding! Troy Coldbrook ain't the man to take something don't belong to him."

"But, so they'll be no further misunderstanding," Coldbrook added sharply, "I'm serving notice now: Nobody else better get any ideas, either, about Abel Gannon's grass. Long as he's laid up like this, it's everybody hands off. Is that clear?"

"Naturally," Steve Benson said crisply. "There's no call even to raise the point. . . ."

Coldbrook gave him a cold stare, and then with a shrug of one thick shoulder he turned to the door; Wes and Burke Sully, both scowling darkly, joined him there. Hand on the knob, Troy looked back to the sheriff. "Ride part way with us, Tom?"

The man hesitated, then shook his head. "I thought I'd stay here tonight. I've ridden plenty for one day."

Steve Benson asked, "Did you have any luck out at Dead Man, Tom? Find any sign on the holdup?"

"I found sign," the lawman answered sourly. "But nothing I could follow. Afraid I have to write that one off. . . . Tomorrow I mean to get an earlier start, hunting the pair you and Joe Niles figure were here today. Doc's not satisfied, and neither am I, that everything's just the way it looks."

Troy Coldbrook looked from one face to another. He demanded sharply, "What's all *this* about? What are you hinting at?"

"Why, maybe it was no accident, Troy. Looks almost as though a couple of range tramps might have stopped by, maybe jumped the old fellow when he caught them ransacking the place looking for a cache or something—thought they'd killed him and tried to cover up. Might not be like that at all, of course, but it needs to be investigated."

Troy Coldbrook scowled over this suggestion. Benson, who had been watching his son, wondered if it was really true or only imagination that he surprised Wes in an expression of guilty alarm. His eyes hardened with cold suspicion.

But he kept it to himself.

He told the sheriff, "I'll be over myself, Tom. I'd kind of like to help you look, if there's no objection. I want to see this thing through."

73

Tom Fawcett stroked his silky mustache, with thumb and forefinger. "That's fine with me," the lawman said. "I can always use an extra pair of eyes."

Steve Benson nodded. "I'll be here. . . ."

It was not far short of midnight when Keystone offsaddled at the home ranch corral. Troy Coldbrook swung down with a tired man's stiffness, that showed his age. He turned his horse over to a member of the crew and walked with a stiff stride to where Wes and Burke Sully and one of his punchers, Vic Gilmore, stood talking; they turned, falling into silence as he came up.

His face looked bleak in the yellow glow of a lantern burning on a corral post. Troy had maintained an ominous quiet during the long ride home, but it was hardly to be expected that he would let this day's fiasco go without giving someone a bad time.

Wes, trying to forestall him, blurted an apology: "I'm sorry, Pa. I guess we kind of messed things up. I'm glad old man Gannon ain't dead, though."

Troy silenced him with the wave of a hand; it turned out that he had entirely different matters on his mind. "About that woman—"

The young man blinked. "Woman? What woman, Pa?"

"I guess I didn't tell you—this other business knocked it clean out of my head. Well, there's some female in town, with a baby. She claims it's yours."

"Mine?" The exclamation was jarred out of Wes Coldbrook, in a tone of pure shock. "Why, that—that's a damn lie!"

The old man shrugged, inside the blanket coat. "Her name's Farrell, or some such. She says it's her sister's kid. She's from Denver—came in on the train this morning. . . ."

Burke Sully was staring at Wes, with a look of intrigued speculation; it was the puncher, Vic Gilmore, who exclaimed suddenly: "That must have been the dame Steve Benson brought back with him!"

Troy snapped a look at his man. "Benson?"

"Sure. They were together—me and Laredo was watching him walk her up from the depot, to the hotel. I made a little joke to Laredo, and Benson overheard me and the bastard whopped me." He felt his jaw, that bore a dark stain of bruise.

Suddenly Wes had a hold of his father's arm. "Pa, that explains everything. It's Benson! He's nothing but a troublemaker—and now he's trying to frame me so he can blackmail us. He'd do something like that; he'd do anything, to make the Coldbrooks look bad in front of the county!"

Troy Coldbrook considered the young man, narrowly. "And there ain't any truth in it? What this woman says?"

"Hell, no!" Wes exploded. "No telling where Benson picked her up, or what she's being paid to put on this act!"

Satisfied, the old rancher nodded. "I ain't opposed to a young fellow sowing his oats—wouldn't be no son of mine, if you didn't have a few high spirits that needed to work themselves out. But, I knew all I had to do was ask and you'd tell me the truth. As for this woman, I told her to be on tomorrow's train, back to Denver."

"Don't worry, Pa. This thing's aimed at me, and I'll take care of it. If she's still in town tomorrow, I'll see she's sent packing. . . ."

Troy turned and started for the main house with his solid, saddleweary stride. Vic Gilmore had already started away, leading his horse to the night corral; Wes Coldbrook thought he was alone until he heard Burke Sully move up beside him. "So!" the foreman said in dry amusement. "Your chickens are flocking home."

Wes turned on him angrily. "You mean, that woman and her brat? I already said they got nothing to do with me!"

"Don't give me that! Maybe you were too drunk to remember, the night you told me all about the little filly you had in Denver last year. Real gone on you, wasn't she? Boy! She *must* have been!"

75

"Shut up!" Wes exploded, in scared fury. "You breathe a word of this to Pa, or anybody else—"

The foreman's voice turned ugly. "Yeah? And why should I do you any favors? Damn it, I ain't gonna forget the way you made me the goat today—laying it onto me, for saying Abel Gannon was dead when he wasn't!"

"I didn't mean to do that," Wes said sullenly. "I had to come up with some kind of a yarn, fast. I never thought the old man would take it the way he did."

"The hell you didn't! It was deliberate—trying to make me look bad, and cover up for your own stupidity!

"And just what happens," Burke Sully went on, "when Gannon comes to his senses, and tells the sheriff what really happened out there this morning? Attempted murder, is how the law will see it. What's Tom Fawcett gonna do about *that?* Worse yet—what's your pa gonna do?"

Leaving that thought to sink home, Burke Sully started to turn away. Wes Coldbrook's voice choked. "Wait! You can't just walk out on me. Don't forget—you're in this too!"

"Damn it, do you think I could forget?" Sully glared at him. "Just don't get the idea you're going to push *that* off on me, too! If the sheriff ever asks, you can believe me I'll tell him exactly who it was swung that gunbarrel!"

Burke Sully punched Wes, not gently, on the shoulder with his fist. "So—you better start thinking, boy," he said. "You better start thinking hard!" And he walked away and left him with it; the crunch of his boots faded in the darkness. He left Wes trembling with the crawl of cold sweat down his ribs.

X

It was soon evident that Benson and the sheriff would have no luck, following sign of the mysterious pair of riders who had been at Gannon's yesterday. Whoever they were, they acted like men who didn't want to be followed. They had picked a tough route for themselves, cutting into a steep rockslide area where shale fragments shifted and rolled treacherously under a horse's hoofs, and where shoeprints were completely lost. After nearly an hour of futile search, Tom Fawcett had to call it off.

Following yesterday's bright weather the morning had turned out cold and windy, with an overcast of darkbellied clouds that clung to the valley rims and scudded before a buffeting wind. The wind whipped at hatbrims and fretted their horses, as the two men reined in to talk the situation over. "Looks clearer all the time," the sheriff said. "They'd only have bothered hiding their trail like this, for good reason. They figured they were leaving murder behind them!"

"Unless it really was an accident, and they knew they'd be blamed."

The sheriff acknowledged the possibility. "Whatever it was," he concluded, "we're not likely ever to know the truth unless Gannon tells us, himself. This trail is getting us nowhere. . . ."

They rode slowly back down to the ranch, and found it deserted. Doc Andrews had decided he would have to risk the move of taking the hurt man into town and had done so that morning with Gannon still unconscious and bedded down as securely as possible in the back of his rig. The buildings seemed almost as though they had stood empty for a year, instead of a matter of a few hours. Even the voice of the hound was missing—Rufe Waller had taken the animal home with him the night before, to keep while they waited to learn if Abel Gannon would recover.

The sheriff returned to town and Steve Benson busied himself with the final chores in closing things up. Finished, he latched the doors carefully against predators and rode home, fighting a mood of depression.

His own place lay north and west, on the flats below the valley escarpment. Headquarters consisted of a low-roofed, two-room house of board-and-batten, a barn and corrals and a few storage sheds, all of them built by Joe Niles and himself with their own hands. They had some root crops under wire, and a windmill with an iron tank. It was enough for their present needs and Benson was well enough pleased, on the whole, with what they had accomplished in a period of a mere couple of years.

On the other hand, for some reason, he had never brought Laurel Whitney here. Somehow he hadn't wanted to view the place through her eyes, or have her see him against this background, suspecting that she would have found it crude and depressing. He told himself sometimes it was a good thing he had this incentive to keep driving, keep building; otherwise he might become satisfied to remain just what he was. He had always heard that was what love of a woman was supposed to do for a man—give him ambition and the will to succeed, and make him dissatisfied with the merely good enough. His love for Laurel Whitney was doubtless the best thing in the world for him. . . .

Rufe Waller's horse was in the yard when he rode in now. Rufe had dropped by on his way from Harry York's, where he had found Harry chafing over the inaction caused by his hurt shoulder and fretfully anxious for news. Benson told Rufe and Joe the inconclusive results of the morning's search, and the three of them held a council of war. There seemed nothing to do but mark time while they waited for developments in Abel Gannon's condition.

"I have to go in to the bank this afternoon," Benson told the others. "While I'm there I'll try to find out if the doc has any news."

A week's absence had left him far behind in his share of the ranch work and it was after four o'clock before he reached town—past closing time. But Benson rode directly to the bank and Dan Whitney himself unlocked the doors for him. Benson went into Whitney's private office and explained his business.

"My problem, Dan," he said as he brought out a manila envelope and laid it on the desk, "is that I've got no good place to keep a thing like this, while I'm waiting to see whether or not Abel Gannon pulls through. If he does, then this belongs to him. If not, it will have to go back to the bank in Denver. Meanwhile, I'd hate like hell to see anything happen to it."

Daniel Whitney picked up the envelope in his pale, fat hands, opened it and slipped out the draft. As he saw the sizable amount of the figures, his soft mouth pursed and his cheeks turned pink. That, Benson knew, would be embarrassment—remembering the scene, in this very room, when he had made his request for a loan and Dan, rubbing soft palms together and piously shaking his head, had murmured his excuses. Too much money, too little security; too great a risk. . . . And here was the Denver bank's paper, for the full amount, and Benson couldn't deny a small sense of satisfaction at watching Laurel Whitney's father squirm a little.

"Glad you were able to get your loan, Steven," the man forced himself to say with an effort at a smile. "I hope you understand, I wanted to help but I just couldn't see my way to do it. Small town bank like mine lacks the resources of an institution the size they have in Denver."

"It's perfectly all right, Dan," Benson said, letting him off the hook. "I knew you had your reasons. I'd done business before with the Denver outfit; I was pretty sure they'd be willing to carry my note, once I made it plain what I wanted the money for. I had no trouble at all.

"Right now, I'm just wondering if you could put this in the vault for safekeeping. Be a load off my mind if I know it's safe."

"Of course—of course," the banker said quickly. "Be glad to. I'll give you a receipt." He made it out with his own hand, and as Benson pocketed it, Whitney called in the cashier and turned the envelope over to him with instructions for it to be locked in the vault. He took out a large white handkerchief and wiped his moist palms.

"A terrible thing, that happened to Abel Gannon," he

murmured, looking at Benson with Laurel's china-blue eyes. "Just terrible! Have you heard anything more about his condition?"

"I'm on my way to the Doc's from here," Benson said, picking his hat off the desk. Both men rose—the banker, a good deal shorter and several soft pounds heavier than the young man. "If there's any news, I'll drop by the house with it."

Dan Whitney had walked as far as the office door with him. He seemed ill at ease and he said now, "We—uh—might not be home. Martha's been given the evening off. Laurel and I are planning to have dinner at the hotel."

"I might join you there," Steve Benson started to say. But he saw the veil that descended over the banker's stare, the stubborn animosity that dragged down the corners of his mouth; and Benson's own eyes narrowed.

He knew Dan Whitney didn't look with pleasure on his interest in Laurel, being much more inclined to favor Wes Coldbrook as a son-in-law. But there seemed to be something new in Whitney's attitude just now. He had never gone so far to make it bluntly plain, as he was doing now without saying it in words, that Steve Benson's company wasn't really wanted. Benson had a feeling that he would be wiser to let it go and not push the matter.

So he swallowed his anger and his puzzled questions, and finished curtly, "On the other hand, I guess I really ought to be getting back to the ranch. So I'll pass it up this time. Give Laurel my regards; and thanks again for the use of your vault."

He left Daniel Whitney frowning after him, and rubbing that handkerchief absently between his fleshy hands.

The doctor, who was a bachelor, lived alone in a tiny house a block off Coldbrook's main street. For all his years, he kept the place up, being a man inclined to putter. The white paint was new, and the yard held the remains of a summer garden, that was dying back now after the season's first frost. Benson found the old man down on his knees, on the front stoop, replacing a broken plank with one of clean yellow pine. "Man has to keep up with the chores," he said, stiffly getting to his feet and brushing sawdust from his clothing. "Whenever he has the chance."

"How's Gannon?"

The doctor laid his hammer on the porch rail and took his visitor inside. Seth Andrews had fitted out one of the two front rooms as a waiting room for his patients, while the other was his office, with an operating table and a glass-fronted cabinet and shelves of weighty, dusty books; the medicine smells were strong, combined with the reek of old tobacco smoke. Besides the old man's sleeping quarters, there was a kitchen and, at the end of a short hall, another room had been added on, with a slanting roof and a single window opening onto the alley behind the house.

This contained a bed and a chair and dresser and could be used, when occasion demanded, as an emergency ward. It was here that the doctor led Steve Benson and showed him his patient, lying with eyes closed and motionless except for the unnatural, heavy breathing.

Benson had hoped for better than this. He asked, "You been able to see any change?"

"None to speak of. He's holding his own—that's about as much as I'd care to say." Andrews rubbed a hand across his bald spot. "I'm keeping a close eye on him, don't dare leave him alone more than a few minutes at a time. Been lucky so far—no emergencies today. But if he don't show some indication of fighting out of that coma, I'm afraid I'll have to have some help. I can't stay this close all the time."

"Troy Coldbrook said to get whatever you needed, and send him the bill. He meant it, too, I think."

"I reckon. . . . Well, we'll see."

Benson thanked him and they went back through the house; on the stoop Doc Andrews picked up his hammer.

He tilted his head on one side, peering at his visitor as the chill autumn wind blew against them and rattled the weeds in the dying flowerbed.

"Supposing there should be news—you going to be in town awhile, in case I want to get in touch with you? At the hotel, maybe?"

"I got to be getting back out to the ranch," Steve Benson told him, as he'd told the banker. He was a few steps down the path toward the gate in the picket fence, and his waiting horse, when something in Andrews's question halted him and pulled him around. "What made you say that?" he asked curiously. "About the hotel . . . What business would I be having there?"

The old man gave him a quizzical look, then shrugged. "Why, none, I guess. Just trying to think where I might be apt to get in touch with you."

"I'll try to get in again tomorrow," Benson said. "Take good care of your patient." He mounted and rode down the hill toward Main.

The wind was rising, clouds overhead dropping lower and putting a premature dusk over Coldbrook town. Though it was early, lamps were already being lighted. The wind scoured the long street, fanning gritty dust and a freight of dry brown leaves ahead of it.

The wind bowled past him and nearly plucked the hat from his head. Two townswomen came along with packages in their arms, their heels clicking on the cement sidewalk. They were hurrying home to their kitchens, to the respectable labors of respectable housewives. Their voices carried clearly to Steve Benson.

"Oh, yes—she's still here! I declare it's a perfect scandal! Apparently she doesn't care at all what anybody says, or thinks. She was told to leave; she was told to get out of that hotel room. But she hasn't done either one. Why, I understand she's even been going around town looking for *work*— walking right into the stores and business places, carrying that child with her for everyone to see! The creature's completely shameless. . . ."

As they went on out of hearing, the other woman was clucking her tongue in shocked agreement. Slowly Steve Benson straightened, took his boot down and shoved it into the stirrup. He felt cold with fury.

It could only be one person they were talking about; and though he had to admit he really knew little about her, he had seen enough to convince him that these gossiping women were utterly wrong. He was put in mind suddenly of a couple of other things—of banker Whitney's vagueness and stiffness of manner when he mentioned Laurel, of Doc Andrews and his cryptic suggestion of Benson's possible interest at the hotel. It must be part of the gossip, he realized suddenly, that he had something to do with Ruth Faris, who defied the town by her mere presence in it. Certainly Laurel had jumped to the conclusion, yesterday morning. Benson turned cold at thought of the gossip she must be hearing now!

But at the moment, he found it was Ruth Faris who concerned him the most. He still owed her something, for her courage and consideration at the time of the holdup at Dead Man. Benson deliberately pulled around and went downstreet again, in the direction of *Coldbrook House.*

Lamps were burning in the lobby and in a number of rooms. Gusty wind made the swinging sign creak faintly with a rhythmic sound. Dismounting, Benson glanced up toward the row of windows along the second story front; thus, he happened to be looking right at them when a woman's piercing cry suddenly sounded, and the figure of a man stumbled backward against one of those squares of glass and knocked it out in an explosion of splintered shards.

The man's back and shoulders showed briefly in the opening. He grabbed at the frame to keep himself from hurtling through, as tinkling glass showered the street below. Benson heard his bellow of anger. Then he disappeared again, into the room. And almost without thinking—merely dropping the reins across the much-chewed tie pole—Steve Benson was ducking the rail and going up the wide steps of the hotel porch at a reaching run.

XI

IT HAD BEEN an exasperating day for Wes Coldbrook. It seemed as though his father had been making notes for a lecture on his shortcomings and failings during his year of managing Keystone, and Troy had chosen this of all days to deliver it. Wes was kept at his heel during most of the afternoon, forced to listen meekly to criticism when, all the time, his nerves were screaming with the torment of a dozen anxieties.

Able to get free at last, he went looking for Burke Sully but couldn't find him. He knew the foreman had been sent with a crew that morning to move Keystone's beef back off Horseshoe Meadow, and there was no telling on what part of the range to look for him now. It really didn't matter, Wes thought, feeling sorry for himself. Sully had made it plain enough, last night, that he would get no help or any sympathy there. Wes Coldbrook had been the author of his own troubles; now he would have to get out of them alone.

He ordered a horse saddled, without saying anything to his father. On a final thought, he went to his room in the big ranchhouse and got his gun, checking the loads carefully before settling belt and holster about his waist. He went out and mounted and took the town trail, under a blustery sky.

There were two worries eating him and he didn't know which tormented him the worse—Abel Gannon, or the Faris bitch. By the time he reached town they had built into a nagging wish for a drink to buck him up, but he put this firmly aside. He couldn't afford any risk of letting go in alcoholic incompetence, before he had found out just how matters stood. So he rode first to the Coldbrook House for a talk with George Meeks, knowing the hotel manager was

84

the biggest gossip in town and could likely tell him what he needed to know.

Meeks was just coming out of his office as Wes walked into the lobby. The man was instantly on the defensive, blinking behind his glasses as he told Troy Coldbrook's son, in a stammering voice, "I'm sorry! I know I promised your father; I *tried* to get her out. But she's paid for a week and she says—"

"She's still here, then?" Wes demanded, cutting in. The other man wagged his head.

"I asked the sheriff—but he agrees that if she won't go, there's no way we can force her to."

Seeing another man frightened and flustered in his presence made Wes Coldbrook feel better. He straightened his shoulders and stood a little taller as he said, with harsh confidence, "*I'll* get her out! Which room?"

"Number five. Upstairs, at the front."

At the steps Wes remembered and turned back to ask, "Any news of Abel Gannon?"

"I hear he's just the same—still unconscious. They say the doctor doesn't give him much chance. It's a terrible thing, isn't it? Just terrible!"

"Yeah," Wes Coldbrook said gruffly, to hide his surging of relief at knowing that here, at least, things were no worse. As long as Abel Gannon didn't recover consciousness and tell the sheriff what had happened in his kitchen yesterday morning, Wes Coldbrook was still safe.

To this other matter, then . . .

He mounted the steps to the second floor, where the corridor was floored with turkey red carpeting, and there were oil lamps in shining brass holders along the walls. Near the head of the stairs he found the door of Number Five, and thought he heard someone moving about. Drawing a breath, he laid his kunckles sharply against the panel.

For just a moment, all sound within the room ceased as though his knock had startled the occupant into motionlessness. Then a step approached the door, a key turned, and the woman stood looking at him. Recognition was immediate, and it was mutual. He saw her shoulders stiffen, saw the cold dislike that instantly shaped her mouth.

"So you actually came! I wondered if you would."

He hadn't expected to feel embarrassment. Now that he faced her, the look in her eye somehow made him uneasy as he recalled, past a remembered haze of drunkenness, what had passed on the only other occasion of their meeting. He covered up for this by affecting a bold front. "Why, sure," he said, making himself grin at her. "You wouldn't prevent a man from seeing his son, would you?"

She made no answer to that, her mouth set firmly. But she drew aside as Wes Coldbrook walked into the room, calmly heeling the door shut behind him. He had already caught sight of the bundle on the bed and he went over for a look. The infant lay quiet, staring solemnly back at him. Wes cuffed the Stetson back from his forehead and stood with knuckles on hips regarding it, for a long minute. "Keeps right on growing, don't he?" he said in a gruff voice.

"He's a fine, healthy baby," Ruth Faris answered. "Not that you care."

That brought him around, scowling at her where she stood near the door. The room was shadowed by the premature dusk outside.

"I'm just wondering," Wes said, "how in hell you tracked me down."

"It was your own doing. If you hadn't come back, two months ago, I doubt if I'd ever have been able. But you made it easy for me—a few questions, asked in the right places—"

He cut her off. "All right! So you found me. More to the point, you found my old man. But you've wasted your time. I can tell you now, you'll get no payoff."

"Do you really think that's why I'm here—for money?" She seemed to be having trouble with her breathing, and her voice trembled a little. "If all I had wanted was to blackmail you," she said tensely, "or to hurt you with your

86

father, there are ways I could have done that. For one thing, I wouldn't have held back from telling him just what happened the first time we met—what you tried to do. . . ."

Wes felt the heat spread upward through his throat, into his cheeks, and suddenly he couldn't look at her. That was one thing he had never told Burke Sully—the sordid sequel to his little escapade of a year ago. His memory of it was blurred by an alcoholic haze, but the sense of it was clear enough: Two months ago, in Denver again, he'd oiled up and against his own better judgment had gone around to look up the girl he'd amused himself with the summer before. This time his luck had run out. The girl was dead—a development he had never dreamed of—and instead there was this sister to confront him and, when she learned who he was, to charge him with being the father of the dead woman's child.

All that was bad enough; what appalled him was the vague recollection of what had happened next. He'd been drunk; he'd gone to that house with only one thing in mind, and he was never a man who liked to be thwarted. And there had been this other girl, easily as desirable as the one he'd come to see. . . .

He shrugged and roughened his voice to cover his confusion. "All right!" he muttered. "Maybe I made kind of a fool of myself, that day. But, nothing came of it. I never hurt you any," he insisted, coloring even more at the thought of this slight figure of a woman holding him at bay and finally sending him packing. He added harshly, "If you try to tell my pa any different, it won't do you a damn bit of good."

Color touched her own cheeks, heightening her attractiveness—even in his present mood he didn't fail to notice. "Don't worry about that!" she snapped. "I'm no more anxious to have anyone know about it, than you are! I've told your father exactly what it is I'm asking—for you Coldbrooks to admit you have a responsibility to that baby there on the bed. That is, if you have any decency. . . ."

For just a moment, her intensity and his own conscience battered hard against Wes Coldbrook. But worse than any feeling of shame was the one ultimate necessity—his fear of his pa. After what Troy had said about the woman and her charges against him, Wes knew that he could never bear for the old man to know the truth. So much was certain.

Combined with the nagging worry about Abel Gannon, all this built up an intolerable pressure. A trickle of cold sweat broke and ran down his ribs; his chest swelled. He felt his hands ball into aching fists.

"There's nothing I can do," he said flatly. "Even if you'd take money, I haven't got any. You can't do anything here but make a nuisance of yourself. We want you out of town—and first of all, we want you out of this hotel. I'm here to make sure you go."

She defied him. "I won't!"

"We'll see about that!"

He looked about. A couple of suitcases stood in a corner of the room. Wes Coldbrook went and picked one of them up, put it on the bed and opened it. He walked to the closet door, flung it open. The closet held little enough—a dress and a coat, on hangers, and a hat on a nail. Wes got them, threw them into the suitcase. After that he strode to the dresser that stood against one wall of the room, where he pulled open a drawer, finding it filled with the baby's things. He started to lift them out—the next moment a fury descended on him, the articles were snatched from his hands. "You leave those alone!" Ruth Faris cried.

Coldbrook, angry now, dropped a hand upon her shoulder. His touch seemed to release a tiger. She whirled, sliding out from under his fingers, and her own hands came against his chest and shoved him away with a strength surprising in one so much smaller. He had a glimpse of furious, blazing eyes in a frightened face. Then, as he tried to catch his balance, a bootheel caught on the edge of the carpet. He was spun about, arms flailing. His hat fell from his head.

He heard a cry of alarm from the girl as he fell against the window and one shoulder, with all his weight behind it, struck the pane solidly.

Wes felt the glass go out with a smash. He flung his arms wide, managed to clutch at the frame and keep from going through the opening, while the material of his heavy coat saved him from being hurt on the shards of glass still clinging to the frame. But it was a near thing and for a moment neither of them moved—he gasping and startled; Ruth Faris staring in alarm as she saw what had nearly happened.

Then Wes Coldbrook heaved himself away from the window, getting his balance again. "Why, damn you!" he exclaimed.

Cold air swirled in through the smashed window. At what she saw in Wes Coldbrook's face, the woman lost color and fell back a step; he paced after her, holding his voice steady with an effort. "You've caused too much trouble already. How much more do you think we'll put up with? What good can you do yourself, defying my pa and me?"

Ruth Faris lifted her head; her eyes were a dark stain against the pallor of her cheeks. "I'm not afraid of you," she answered, but her voice quavered slightly.

"What do you think you can prove?" he went on harshly. "Do you have some idea you can maybe convince the town, and turn it against the Coldbrooks—something like that? Why, we *are* the town! Nobody will ever do anything but what we tell them," he boasted. "No one would dare!"

"I'm not trying to turn anyone against anything," she answered. Suddenly there was a shine of tears in her eyes and her lips trembled. "It just isn't fair!" she cried, her voice breaking. "No one should have such special privileges that when they wreck something—like a human life—they don't even have to stop and—and pick up the pieces!"

Suddenly she was crying, her mouth pulled out of shape, and the bitter tears shining on her cheeks. Wes stared at her, appalled and then furious.

"Now listen!" he blurted, and got no response, no indication she even heard. His mouth hardened. "I said, *listen!*" He reached and grabbed her wrist; at once she screamed and began fighting him, tearing at his hand with her fingers. Wes swore and twisted her arm fiercely. In his anger a hand rose, cocked for a blow. "You'll only make things worse for yourself!" he said harshly. "Nobody's going to hear you, or pay any attention even if they—"

His words broke off as boots struck in the corridor and someone shouldered the door. It slammed open, struck the wall and rebounded. Jerking around, Coldbrook saw Steve Benson framed in the doorway.

XII

THE TWO MEN STARED. Benson was the first to find his voice; he said coldly, "I think you'd better let go of her, Wes!" Ruth Faris gave another pull against the hand that held her wrist, and this time Coldbrook released his grip and she stumbled back from him.

For a moment after that there was no movement except for the curtains at the smashed window, stirring on the cold draft the opening of the door had created. Steve Benson, breathing a little heavily from his hurried climb of the stairs, pulled off his hat as he turned to the woman. He said, "I thought you might need some help . . ."

She was rubbing her wrist with her other hand; she looked white and scared. She glanced at Coldbrook, and touched her tongue to her lower lip. "I—think I'll be all right now," she said, faltering. "Mr. Coldbrook's just leaving."

"Maybe he is and maybe he isn't!" Wes retorted. He had got over his initial surprise and now there was speculation in the look he put on these two. "Maybe we're going to get a few things straightened out, while we're all together."

"What makes you think we have anything to talk about?" Steve Benson snapped.

"Why, that should be plain enough—if it wasn't before. I told Pa it was something like this. You'd do anything to hit at the Coldbrooks. It couldn't be any coincidence, you coming back from Denver on the same damned train with this female!"

A puzzled frown settled over Steve Benson's face. The other man's words pulled him further into the room, to a stand directly before Wes Coldbrook. Benson said coldly, "I got no idea in the world what you're hinting at. But it's a solid fact I never laid eyes on the young lady, before we happened to wind up in the same day coach."

Wes Coldbrook's lips quirked, took on a hard-edged sneer. "I guess we're supposed to believe that! Practically a whole week you had in Denver—plenty of time for the pair of you to cook this up. And no telling what else went on between you. Likely she's no better than her slutty sister . . ."

He got no further than that. Steve Benson's hard fist came over and knocked the words back into his teeth, sent Coldbrook reeling and dropped him sprawling across the bed. The baby, startled, loosed a terrified wail. Ruth Faris gasped and hastily ran to snatch it up from the tumble of blankets and clutch it to her.

Wes wasn't really hurt, but after the bounce of the springs rocked him back to a sitting position he stayed where he was, on the edge of the bed, peering up at Benson in a mixture of anger and surprise. Benson stood watching to see what he would do. "So!" Wes muttered finally, in a swallowed tone. He drew a breath, and with a hand on the brasswork of the bedstead levered himself to his feet. Deliberately be began unhooking the fastenings of his blanket coat. "No man," he told Benson as he did it, "ever had the nerve to lay a fist on me!"

"Has to be a first time for everything, doesn't there, Wes?" He flexed the fingers of the hand that had struck Coldbrook. "I wonder if you think it was *you* people were afraid of—instead of what Troy might have done to them. Well, now, suppose you get out of here—like Miss Faris asked you?"

"She's the one that's getting out!" Wes retorted. "First, though, I'm going to teach you some manners." He slid the coat from his shoulders, let it fall.

Benson shook his head a little. "Don't be a fool, Wes. You'll just end up getting your head busted. You're not Troy—even though you seem to spend most of your time trying to prove different."

Wes Coldbrook's face twisted with ugly rage. He spat a word at Benson that turned the other man's eyes cold as flint. "All right, Wes!" Steve Benson said then, quietly. Unbuckling his gungear he laid belt and holster on a chair seat, and started to undo his windbreaker. He was still working at it when Coldbrook rushed him, catching him with his arms momentarily trapped in the sleeves.

Benson tried to swerve away from the wild fist that Wes flung at him, but it caught him on the side of the head, dazing him and throwing him back against the wall. Again Wes struck, the blow taking him on one shoulder. And Benson, still unable to fight back, simply lowered his head and dived forward off the wall, ramming the other squarely in the chest.

He felt his skull connect and heard the wind driven from Coldbrook's lungs. He had to catch himself, then, for Wes was down—knocked off his feet. That gave Benson a moment to finish whipping off the heavy coat that hampered him, and fling it away.

Ruth Faris, clutching the baby, cried a protest but it went unheard. Wes Coldbrook was on his knees, gasping as he dragged air into his lungs. Angry color turned his cheeks crimson. He spat a curse and came lunging up. They met head on.

If Benson had had any idea that Wes was really soft, he was mistaken. Or maybe it was Coldbrook's reckless fury that made him a tough opponent. He came boring straight in, swinging wildly; nor did Steve Benson pull any punches. A hundred past grievances had exploded here—dozens of irritating slights and differences, climaxed by the events of yesterday, culminating in Wes Coldbrook's attempt to kill him at Horseshoe Meadow, and now in the studied insult to Ruth Faris. Benson hardly felt the weight of Coldbrook's fists, in the keen and brutal pleasure of measuring his own blows, cocking and unleashing them and seeing them land.

He took Coldbrook high on a cheekbone, breaking the skin and starting the eye swelling, and a moment afterward sent him spinning across the room to bring up against a chest of drawers where his arm, reaching for balance, swept the water pitcher to the carpet in a smash of broken china. Coldbrook crouched there as he waited until his head cleared, peering around for Benson through the hair streaming into his face. Now he wiped sweat and blood with a sleeve, and wheeled and started toward his enemy again.

Benson stood and let him come, which may have been a mistake. At the last moment Coldbrook's bent-kneed prowl lengthened to a rushing drive and he was on Benson before the latter was quite set for him. A looping right broke past his defense and he felt it sting and numb him as it smashed against his jaw, carrying his head part way around. He staggered and the edge of the door jamb struck his back. And before he had quite recovered, Wes was after him again.

They were through the door, into the hallway, still trading blows at close quarters. Benson saw a smear of yellow light and felt the heat from an oil lamp in a wall bracket, took warning just as his head was about to smash into it. He jerked aside barely in time, and Wes missed a chopping swing at Benson and drove his own fist into the wall. Steve Benson set himself, braced his shoulders and swung. Coldbrook reeled away under the impact; pushing free of the wall, Benson went after him.

Doors along the corridor had burst open and he glimpsed startled faces. Somewhere in the building voices were shouting in alarm. Benson ignored them all. Wes Coldbrook's bleeding face was in front of him again and he battered aside the warding forearm Wes threw up to check his blow, drove a fist into it. Wes made a frantic effort to duck. Suddenly his eyes widened; his hands clutched at Benson. The latter tried to pull back but Wes had a grip on his shirt that could not be broken, and the next moment the two of them were falling into emptiness.

Benson saw a banister reel past him, like the spokes of a turning wheel; he realized he must have sent Wes Coldbrook backing into the stairwell, and Wes was going down and dragging his opponent with him. He missed a grab at the polished handrail and after that both men hit the stairs, spilling over and over in a tangle.

The hard edge of a riser caught Steve Benson across the middle of the back; one of Coldbrook's boots struck the side of his head. The grip on his shirt was broken but every attempt to brake his tumbling fall came to little. Finally, his long length got wedged between banister and wall and brought him to a halt. He sprawled there, dazed and dizzied. As streaking lamplight circled and settled, he realized he was nearly at the foot of the steps with Wes Coldbrook a huddled lump stirring on the lobby carpet, a few yards distant.

Whatever else it did, their spill down the stairway seemed to have put an end to the fight. Wes Coldbrook, when he hauled himself to his feet, appeared to have had enough; he looked bruised and shaken, and Benson was in pretty much the same condition. George Meeks stood in the door of his office while a cook and a couple of waitresses stared from the hallway leading to the kitchen. Guests, interrupted in their meals, crowded the dining room archway. With a sinking feeling, Benson saw Dan and Laurel Whitney among them.

The banker still had his table napkin tucked into the expanse of his broad waistcoat, a thunderous scowl of disapproval on his fleshy face. Laurel was eying the two disheveled brawlers with a look of disbelief. Now Benson saw her eyes lift to the stairs behind him; he turned—and there was Ruth Faris standing partway down, pale as a ghost, the baby in one arm and her other hand clutching the railing.

Wes Coldbrook, too, realized that he had an audience; it set him to straightening his clothing, trying to gather the rags of his dignity about him. He pushed the hair back from his face, and lifted a trembling finger toward Ruth Faris. "This is final!" he told Benson loudly. "Take that—that woman out of here. Otherwise I have every excuse to order her thrown out!"

"You've got things a little backwards, haven't you?" Benson corrected him. "You're the one went busting in and smashed up her room for her. I'd say it's the hotel's duty to furnish her with another."

"No!" That was Ruth Faris, speaking out in an anguished voice. "Staying here any longer could only make more trouble. I'll find some place else."

Benson was prepared to argue. "The man has no right—" he began, and broke off as he saw the look on her face. Plainly she had taken as much as she could, and was absolutely serious about this. Slowly, then, he nodded. "All right. Pack your things. You have a refund coming on your week's rent. I'll collect it."

She thanked him with a hesitant nod, turned back up the stairs. A glance at Coldbrook got Benson a scowl and shrug. Across a shoulder, Wes growled at George Meeks, "Give him the money."

"Yes sir." The manager hurried around behind his desk, obviously glad enough to have the thing settled for him.

Steve Benson turned to the Whitneys then. He saw Laurel's look of angry hurt; when he made a move in her direction, her father stiffened, took her by the elbow and turned her quickly away. She let Dan Whitney lead her back through the arch into the dining room. After what they had just witnessed, this was hardly the time to try and explain anything.

Benson let it go, turning instead to the desk where George Meeks had hastily set out a small stack of silver dollars. He pocketed them, with a curt nod, and shouldering past Wes Coldbrook climbed the stairs again.

When he came down he had his hat and coat and his gunrig was in place about his hips. He carried Ruth Faris' suitcases, which she had hastily packed; she walked ahead of him, with the baby in her arms and her head high. They crossed the lobby, that was deserted now. And they emerged into a boisterous autumn evening whose cold night wind buffeted the eaves of the town's buildings, and blew ragged clouds across the stars.

The woman turned to Benson to say earnestly, "I'm sorry to have been so much trouble. I do thank you for everything you've done, and especially for getting my money back from the hotel manager. But, you don't have to bother about me any more!"

He shook his head. "Not so fast," he told her. "You need a job, and a place to live. Well, I just had myself an idea. Let me hook these suitcases of yours onto my saddle, and then you come along and we'll see what we can do about this. . . ."

XIII

A GOOD AROMA of frying meat overlaid the usual medicinal smells of Doc Andrews' house. As Benson ushered Ruth Faris inside, the doctor emerged from the kitchen; he was in his shirtsleeves, a dishtowel tied about his waist for an apron and his hands smeared with flour. He blinked at the young woman and the bundle in her arms and said, with professional brusqueness, "Well! What have we here—a sick baby?"

"The youngster's fine, Doc," Benson said, closing the door. "I've brought you someone to help take care of Abel Gannon. She's looking for a job, and a place to stay. And you'll remember Troy Coldbrook said he'd pay the bill."

The old doctor's eyes narrowed; he rubbed a palm across

96

his jaw, leaving a streak of flour there. "I don't reckon," he said shrewdly, "this is quite what Troy had in mind. Not if your young lady is the one I'm thinking she is."

"I can imagine what you're thinking, and what you've probably heard!" Benson cut in, as he saw how Ruth went tense and changed color. "I'm only beginning to piece the thing together myself—but I've got a feeling that once you know the whole story, you may want to do something to help out."

Andrews' look remained darkly skeptical, and Ruth looked at Benson with a shake of her head. "You shouldn't have brought me here. It wouldn't be fair dragging someone else into my troubles, even if he should believe me."

"Now, wait a minute!" The doctor raised a hand, scowling thunderously. "It also ain't fair to rouse an old man's curiosity and then leave him dangling. Now you've started, I reckon you better finish telling me just what— Holy smoke!" he cried, interrupting himself. "My steaks!"

He whirled and went at a rush back into the kitchen. Steve and the girl followed and found him at the cook stove, amid a cloud of smoke and sputtering grease, digging with a spatula at the frypan he held in one hand. He threw a despairing look over his shoulder at Ruth. "Young lady, can you cook?"

She hesitated. "Yes . . ."

"One thing I never learned the knack of, worth a damn. If you can make some kind of sense out of what I've got started here, then you're both welcome to help me eat it, and we can talk at the same time. That is, if you haven't already had dinner."

The other two exchanged a look. "Not me," Benson admitted, and she shook her head.

"I'll be happy to do what I can," Ruth said. "If there's some place I can put the baby . . ."

She was an excellent cook. Even after the start the old doctor had had at ruining the meal, she managed to set out a very presentable array of steak and potatoes and gravy,

97

stewed tomatoes and hot baking-soda biscuits. They ate at the oilcloth-covered table in the kitchen, with the door open leading to the bedroom so that Ruth could instantly hear any sound from the baby that lay asleep on the doctor's own bed. Seth Andrews, for his part, seemed to be constantly alert for any slight sound issuing from the rear room, where Abel Gannon maintained an unbroken, eerie stillness.

Steve Benson himself had no attention for anything but the story the young woman told them. He found himself eating almost mechanically, his appetite lost in growing anger. He had a strong feeling that Ruth was glossing over certain details in telling of Wes Coldbrook's second visit to Denver, after the baby's birth and the death of her sister. But whatever she left out, and for whatever reason, the gist of the story was clear enough; and Benson, looking across the table, could see that Doc Andrews, too, was convinced.

There was a silence, then. Benson picked up his coffee cup, found he had let it go stone cold; but he shook his head when Ruth would have fetched the granite pot, to pour him a fresh cup. "Thanks," he said gruffly. "Somehow I don't seem to be very hungry."

"I know what you mean," Doc Andrews said. "Question is, what are we going to do about this?"

"Now, please! Understand me," Ruth said quickly, "I didn't tell you all this because I was hoping you'd take on my troubles. Only, I—I just had to talk it out with someone. I don't know what way to turn!"

"Those Coldbrooks!" Doc Andrews muttered blackly. "They're a ruthless breed, all right! Troy always figured no one had a right to call him to account for anything he ever did, and he raised Wes to think the same way. Like it don't even matter how you go through life, making messes for other people to have to clean up! Well, the day may come when they both learn different."

Steve Benson's hand, resting on the table, hardened to a fist. "But when?" he demanded in cold fury. "And how?"

"How do we make Wes Coldbrook own up and admit he

fathered that poor little tyke in the other room?" The doctor shook his head slowly. "I don't know. Maybe there isn't any way. I'm an old man, Steve; and I've learned patience, if very little else." He got an ancient cherrywood pipe from his coat pocket, looked into the blackened bowl and fetched up a pocketknife with which to dig it out.

"But at least, we can do what we can to ease things for this young lady. If she's determined to stick it out here, no matter what the town says and does, then she's welcome enough to stay with me. I can use a housekeeper; more particularly, I need someone to help me keep an eye on Abel Gannon, so I can get out and go about my regular business. As you say, Troy Coldbrook offered to pay for it if I needed to hire someone. He may not be too much inclined to, when he finds who it is I hired—but you can damn well bet I'm going to hand him the bill!"

"I don't ask any pay," Ruth said quickly. "Just a roof over our heads for a few days, while I decide whether it's any use staying, or if I just ought to give up and take the baby on back where we came from."

"Do you have folks there in Denver, or anywhere?" Steve Benson asked. "Anyone to help out with him?"

"No, there was only Ellen and me. We'd been on our own since the typhoid took both our parents, three years ago. I've tried to make a home for us, by doing sewing, and clerking in stores. I wanted Ellen to have an education. She was a very bright girl, and very sweet. She was all I had . . ."

Her voice shook and Benson swore under his breath and swung to his feet. Scraping at the bowl of the pipe, Doc Andrews shot a look at him and said quietly, "All right, Steve. Keep a rein on that temper. Won't get you anywhere to lose it. Just what good did your row at the hotel do for you?"

He nodded. "You're right," he agreed, when he had his breathing under control. He started to say more, then closed his lips against it. He realized how much there was that he alone knew or suspected, and that he wasn't free yet to

99

discuss with anyone—the business at Dead Man, and his dark suspicions connected with the clubbing of Abel Gannon. For the time being his hands were as firmly tied as Ruth's.

Steve Benson said bleakly, "For someone as ineffective as Wes Coldbrook, that fellow's piling up a real score against himself! The day is coming when not even all of Troy's power can save him from a reckoning."

Shortly afterward, he was moving on foot through the autumn night and the dark streets, against an occasional gust of wind that came booming around building corners, to catch a man and yank at his clothing and nearly fling him offstride. The town was quiet enough; if the fight at the hotel had caused any disturbance, the excitement had long since died.

From the doctor's little house it was only a couple of short blocks to the imposing residence of the Whitneys. A few lights shone behind the high windows of the sprawling house; Benson's throat was dry with apprehension as he climbed the porch steps. A lamp in the hall picked out the design of the big door's frosted glass window. After he had rung the bell, he waited and presently saw a shadow swim across the glass, growing larger as someone approached. He pulled off his hat and the door swung open. Laurel Whitney stared at him.

He saw how she stiffened. She drew back a step; the door started to close.

"Don't!" he cried in protest.

A ray of lamplight from the wall holder slanted across her cheek now, showing him the angry set of her mouth, but her eyes were still lost in shadow, beneath the bright nimbus of her hair. She spoke in a quick and tense rush of words, as though she were in terrible haste to get them spoken and out of her mouth.

"Steve Benson, I was never so hurt and disappointed and —and disgusted with anyone, in all my life! I think you

100

have unspeakable nerve to come here, after that scene at the hotel. And I wish you'd go away!"

He had known it would be bad, but nothing like this. "Be reasonable!" he exclaimed. "I'm not proud for you to have seen me fighting, but I hoped you'd at least want to hear my side of the thing. Especially as I didn't even start it!"

"*Fighting?*" she echoed, and swung her shoulders in an angry movement. "Oh, well, that was bad enough, of course; but I think you know it's not what I mean. Wes Coldbrook told me what you were fighting about."

Cold anger solidified inside him. "Wes did, did he?"

"Not that I needed him to tell me. Why, it's all over town. About you, and that—that—"

Benson knew then what she had heard, and moreover that she believed it. It was enough to make him shake his head in helpless disappointment. "But it's not true!" he protested. "Ruth Faris and I aren't even friends. She's just someone who did me a favor. . . ."

"That's one thing to call it, I suppose," she snapped. "I certainly know what to call *her*—though I'd never bring myself to use the word! And I think it's just terrible, what the two of you are doing to embarrass Wes Coldbrook and his father!"

For a long moment he could think of nothing to say, while the cold wind boomed in the eaves of the porch and made the lamp flicker in its holder. Slowly, then, Benson shook his head. "Laurel, I hoped we knew each other better than this," he said. "Certainly, if we meant anything to each other, you couldn't be so quick to believe such charges against me!"

She seemed to be crying suddenly, swinging her head from side to side. "Oh, I—I don't know!" she cried. "I just don't know!" From somewhere inside the house came her father's voice, calling her name. Laurel seemed to grasp at the sound. "I have to go now," she said hastily. "I can't—"

And even as he protested, she stepped back and the door swung closed in his face.

Steve Benson stood looking at it, all her incoherent and accusing words swirling through his head. Once he lifted a hand to the bell but let it drop, knowing that she wouldn't answer. There had been a stern finality in the closing of that door; it had sent a lot of dreams toppling and something told him that the job of setting them up again might prove to be too big, if she had no more faith in him than this.

He'd always known she was self-centered—spoiled by her father, with a tendency to unreasoning impulse when something occurred to hurt her feelings. But this had been more than a lovers' quarrel.

He finally turned from the dark blank face of the door; pulling on his hat, he tramped down the porch steps and the flagstone path to the gate.

So much time and emotion had been invested in this relationship, and in all his hopes for the future, that he felt now like a ship cut adrift. Well, he would just have to pull himself out of this mood, after its first numbing shock.

He was walking back down the hill, his thoughts so preoccupied that he had no idea of danger. But as he stepped into the dark mouth of an alleyway, a sound that could have been the scraping of bootleather on cinders reached him above the noise of the wind, and so close at hand that it startled him and made him draw back quickly against the corner of a shed. There he pushed the skirt of his blanket coat aside and laid a hand on the butt of his holstered gun. A shoulder pressed against clapboards, he held his breath and waited for whatever sound he'd heard to be repeated.

A long minute passed, a roweling impatience made him call out sharply, "Is there anyone there?" at the same time drawing the gun.

When he got no answer he moved out, taking the alley mouth in three long strides and whirling as he reached a stretch of high board fence. With gun held ready, he waited again. However briefly, he'd made a target of himself and

102

hadn't drawn fire. Now his mouth pulled out long and he swore under his breath.

Nerves, he decided—nothing more.

At last, shoving his gun back into leather, he turned and walked on down the slant of the hill, convinced that imagination and the restless wind had played a trick on him.

Back in the shadows Wes Coldbrook stood and cursed the trembling that made the gun in his hand shake uncontrollably, while his teeth chattered despite every effort of clenched jaw muscles to hold them still. The chill of the night, the unbearable tension, the raw chagrin of a wasted opportunity all combined to punish him as he heard Benson's footsteps fade.

What the hell was the matter with him? It should have been an easy chance to rid himself of an enemy who seemed, to Coldbrook, bent on plaguing him and thwarting his will at every single turn. But the gun in his hand had wobbled so that he couldn't draw a steady aim, not even when Benson had moved directly across his sights. And so he'd let the moment pass, and now it was too late.

The worst of it was that his failure of nerve had left him hopelessly shaken, and drenched with an icy sweat; it had drained off hoarded stores of courage, that he had been anxiously nursing with the help of the bottle in his coat pocket—courage he needed for an even more difficult job he had ahead of him.

This was a job no one else but himself could do. It had to be faced—before the night was much older. It set his gut to crawling just to think of it.

XIV

As BENSON WAS turning in again at the doctor's house, hoofbeats thudded the dust and four riders drifted up through the windy dark. He made out his partner, Joe Niles, and

Sam Tremaine and Rufe Waller of the Pool. The fourth rider was Tremaine's seventeen-year-old, Tommy, who duplicated exactly his father's lean features and mild brown eyes. They drew to a halt facing Benson.

"The boys were all at our place," Niles said, "and we figured we just had to know about Abel Gannon. Figured we'd ride on in and learn for ourselves if there was any news. How is he?"

"No change, up to an hour ago," Benson told them. "I don't think Doc gives him much of a chance—not when he's been in a coma this long, without any break. But, come on in and we'll see what he says now."

Joe Niles detected something in his partner's manner, for he came abreast of Benson on the porch steps and delayed long enough to take him by an elbow and ask, in a low voice, "You all right, Steve?"

"All right," he said briefly. He had a few bruises, picked up in the fight at the hotel, but mostly he was aware of a numbness left from the scene with Laurel; this seemed a climax to the whole crazy series of events that had had their inception at Dead Man Summit, two nights ago. He added, "You didn't happen to stop anywhere over town, on your way in?"

"Why no. We came straight to the doc's. Why—has something been going on?"

"You might call it that." Benson spoke dryly. "But it can wait. Let's go in the house."

Andrews said, "Come on in, boys." He stood aside as they filed past, and closed the door shutting away the crisp night.

They nearly filled the Doc's waiting room; there weren't chairs enough so they stood—a solemn, harried group of men, listening while Seth Andrews reaffirmed what Benson had already said. "I'm worried," he told them frankly. "Nearly thirty-six hours, now, he's been like that—still breathing, still alive, but without any sign at all of rousing. The longer it goes on this way, the less I like it."

104

Rufe Waller said heavily, "I guess there really wasn't any point in our coming in. Certainly nothing we can do, to change matters." Sam Tremaine added, "A man feels so damned useless, just waiting around for word."

"You don't feel much more useless than I do," Andrews assured him bitterly. "All these years I been his friend, and now I'm damned if I know one single thing to do for him. Me, that's supposed to be a doctor!"

A movement drew Steve Benson's eye to the hall doorway; there he discovered Ruth Faris with the sleeves of her blouse rolled to the elbows and her hands twisted in a towel. As soon as she saw his eyes on her she drew hastily back. For some reason he felt compelled to follow her.

She stood in the center of the kitchen, facing him with a look of some confusion. "Why did you run away?" he asked her.

"I didn't want to seem to be putting my nose in other people's business," she exclaimed. She raised a hand tiredly and pushed the hair from her forehead. The evidences of industry were all around them; the dinner things had been put away and now she appeared to be in the middle of a washing. Kettles of water were boiling on the stove. There was a tub and a scrub board that the doctor must have turned up somewhere. It hadn't occurred to Benson how much washing a baby made necessary; and this was the first chance Ruth had had since she came to Coldbrook.

She said, "Those are your friends, aren't they? The other members of your 'Pool'."

It made him blink. "How did you know about that? I don't think I ever mentioned them."

"See what I mean, about sticking my nose in?" she said, and smiled a little. "I'm sorry . . . Anyway, I was talking to Dr. Andrews, after you left this evening. He told me something of what you're trying to do, and how this Mr. Gannon being hurt had upset all your hopes. I was awfully sorry to hear it, Steve. Especially since all I seem to have done, by being here, is make still more trouble for you with the Cold-brooks. Believe me, I never intended to!"

He couldn't answer. Looking at her earnest frown, he was suddenly overwhelmed by the contrast between this girl and Laurel Whitney. In the short time he had known her, her whole concern had been for others—for the baby, for Benson and his friends. Never once did she seem to be thinking of herself. With Laurel, on the other hand, he could scarcely remember a time when she thought about anything else.

As they stood together here, neither speaking, Doc Andrews suddenly shouted, "Abel Gannon's stirring! I just heard movement, back in his room . . ."

Quickly Benson wheeled and started after the doctor, and Ruth followed down the long, narrow hall leading to the separate room that had been tacked on to the back of the house to serve Andrews as a sick ward. The faint glimmer from a single turned-down lamp showed beyond the half-closed door at its end. Andrews pushed this door wide and, moving up behind him, Benson saw past his shoulder the dim outline of the man beside the bed, leaning over Abel Gannon's prone shape with something in his hands. The man's head swung toward the door; he showed them the face of Wes Coldbrook.

For a long heartbeat the scene froze that way. Benson was aware of Ruth Faris, pressing close at his back. He had time to notice the open window, and to guess it was some sound Coldbrook had made raising it and crawling through that must have reached Seth Andrews' alert ear.

Wes Coldbrook, the first to break free of surprise, was the first to move. He lifted whatever it was he held and flung it straight at the doorway, and the three who crowded there ducked instinctively. It was only a pillow from the bed. It struck the wall softly, and dropped; but the surprise of it gave Coldbrook a second's advantage and he used this to turn and make a dive for the open window.

Belatedly Steve Benson roused himself. He shouted Cold-brook's name and, elbowing Andrews aside, plunged for-

106

ward. Wes fumbled his gun up and his bullet struck the door frame. Benson's horror at the thought of danger to Ruth made his hand shake as he dug for his own weapon. At his shot the mingling of the two explosions was deafening, trapped in the small room. But he was sure he hit Coldbrook; Wes fell back against the window frame, as though he had been pushed. He was still on his feet, however, and with his left arm held stiffly against his side he turned and flung a leg across the sill. In a violently contorted movement he managed to squirm across, ducking his head and shoulders through the opening, and a second later dropped from sight into outer darkness.

Benson reached the window only a second later. As he pawed the curtains aside, chill night wind breathed in at him and, in the black alley behind the house, a gun promptly smeared the night with muzzle flame; a bullet chewed into the siding, close enough to make him pull his head back. Out there running footsteps spurted, quickly fading. He did not waste a second bullet from his own gun.

The room behind him was suddenly alive with voices as the others came crowding. Doc Andrews stood holding the pillow Wes Coldbrook had thrown. He said in angry disbelief, "He meant to smother him—must have hoped to make it look like he just stopped breathing. . . ."

"But who was it?" Joe Niles demanded.

"Young Coldbrook," Steve Benson snapped. He was already seated on the windowsill, ready to drop through. "I think I got him in the shoulder—there's blood, here on the windowframe."

"But—Coldbrook!" one of the others exclaimed. "*Why?*"

"What's the difference, why?" Niles retorted. "Ask him that when we've caught him. You, Tommy," he said, turning to Sam Tremaine's boy. "Run see if you can locate the sheriff. The rest of you, come on—before he gets clean away from us!"

He whirled to lead the chase back down the hall to the kitchen and the alley door. Benson saw Ruth staring at him;

her face looked pale and scared in the dim light. She cried impulsively, "Be careful, Steve!" He nodded, and dropped through the opening, into weeds and cinders.

He listened a moment, then started forward as the kitchen door flung open and the other Pool members came bursting out. "This way, I think!" Benson called, and led them off at a sprinting run. He was thinking no further than a hard determination that, while they had Coldbrook wounded and afoot, they must not let up on him.

It really could not have been very much later, though the listening and the waiting made it seem so, when Ruth Faris heard the doctor's sharp voice calling her. She had forced herself to return to her work in the kitchen and was mechanically going through the motions, still shaken by the events of this terrifying evening. Quickly she straightened from the washtub and wiping her hands, hurried down the hall into Abel Gannon's room. Seth Andrews leaned over the bed. "The lamp!" he exclaimed, gesturing. She turned up the wick, and as its golden light brightened, she looked again—and saw Abel Gannon's eyes wide open, the eyeballs glistening twin reflected spots of light.

Seth Andrews bent closer and, moving toward the bed, Ruth heard the murmur of the old man's voice. The doctor answered him: "Now, it's all right, Abel. You're at my place. You've had you a bad knock on the head. No—better lie still," he added as Gannon made some feeble move to raise himself.

The hurt man dropped back, groaning. "It hurts!" He said it almost in surprise.

"Sure—sure." Andrews touched his shoulder. "So you just take it easy a little!"

Ruth, suppressing her excitement, exclaimed, "Why, he's really better, isn't he? He's going to be all right!"

But then she saw the stabbing look the old doctor lifted to her, and the words died on her tongue. It was a bleak, angry look of utter hopelessness, and it left her openmouthed and bewildered. Abel Gannon, for his part, didn't seem even aware of her presence. He continued to peer into his old friend's face as Andrews, making his eyes carefully expressionless, turned again to him. "Do you remember anything about what happened, Abel? How it was you got hurt?"

The man in the bed frowned in puzzlement. "No," he said slowly. "That's funny. I don't remember nothing."

"You were found lying on the ground behind your house, yesterday morning," Andrews said, gently prodding. "Next to the woodstack. It had fallen over." Gannon seemed to be struggling to pierce the fog, but his face held no recollection. Andrews persisted: "Looked like you'd had some company. A couple of riders. We found tracks; and there was coffee poured, sitting out on the table. And your shotgun in the middle of the floor . . ."

He broke off. A new, fleeting expression had crossed the old man's face—a look of remembrance, as though these details were clues that pierced the mist. Suddenly a fierce light kindled in the sunken eyes; the colorless lips stirred.

"Coldbrook!"

Ruth drew nearer, her eyes moving from Gannon's face to Doctor leaning above him. "What about Troy Coldbrook?" the doctor demanded sharply.

"No, no. The boy—Wes. And Burke Sully. It was them! They was trying to pressure me, trying to make me say I'd sell out to them instead of to Benson. And finally, I think it was—yeah! It was Wes that grabbed me. Sully was clear across the room, watching out the window. He said there was somebody coming. . . ."

"That's all you remember?"

"I—I guess. No wait a minute! I recall gettin' mad and reachin' for my shotgun, to order 'em both off the place. Young Coldbrook grabbed it away from me—" The light of memory faded. "That's—all. . ."

"It's enough!" Seth Andrews said bleakly, and straightened. Ruth was suddenly aware that she had stopped breathing. Almost painfully, she filled her lungs.

Gannon said, "Seth! Be honest with me. How bad hurt am I? Am I dying?"

"Why, what are you talking about?" The doctor exclaimed—a little too heartily, Ruth thought. "You ain't scarcely hurt none at all. Skull as hard as yours takes more than a little crack like that, to dent it."

The other moved his head a little on the pillow. "I don't think so. I think I'm hurt pretty damn bad. I don't reckon I got much longer. And here I ain't even made out a will. . . . You got paper on you, Seth? And a pen, maybe?"

"Plenty of time to be thinking of wills!" Andrews said. But his voice sounded a little unsteady, and Ruth saw he was already reaching for a pocket of his coat. He brought out a notebook, a reservoir pen; clearing his throat he added, "But if it'll make you feel easier . . ." He started to uncap the pen.

"Thanks," the hurt man closed his eyes. His face looked crumpled, and as bloodless as the sheet. His voice sounded fainter. "You'll have to write it for me, and then let me sign it. I dunno how to make it sound legal, but maybe you can put in the whereases and the whyfors. Just say that—havin' no kin that I know of—I want my spread to go to Steve Benson. For services rendered, as well as other damn good reasons. Write it, Seth!"

"All right." Andrews flipped through the book until he found a blank page. His pen was poised over it when Ruth exclaimed suddenly, "Doctor!"

He looked sharply at the face of his friend. It had changed. Abel Gannon's eyes, wide open, seemed to be riveted on a spot high in one corner of the room, and they had taken on a strange light. "Jenny!" he said, quite clearly, to the empty air.

Then the light behind his eyes withdrew and the mouth went slack. Doc Andrews' own face deepened to a look of bitter sadness. Deliberately, he recapped the pen and closed the book and returned them both to his pocket. He searched for a pulse. Slowly, the doctor straightened.

110

"He's gone."

Ruth shook her head, shocked and utterly puzzled. "But I don't understand! He seemed so much better. He woke—and he talked to us. . . ."

"I know. I've seen this happen before. During the war, once—a soldier that had half his brain shot away by a minnie ball. Just as he was dying he come to, and he talked so clear you would have thought, those last few minutes, there was nothing the matter with him at all. I've never heard an explanation—one that made any sense."

After a moment, she said, "Jenny was his wife?"

Seth Andrews swallowed, and nodded. Slowly he leaned to draw the sheet up over Abel Gannon's lifeless face.

Another thought occurred to her suddenly. "He never even got to sign his will!"

"Doesn't matter," Andrews told her. "There was two witnesses. You and me. That's an oral will, and it's legal; any court in the land will honor it." He wagged his head.

"So, girl, what we just seen and heard makes Steve Benson the heir to Gannon's spread. And it makes young Coldbrook a murderer!"

XV

LAUREL WHITNEY thought at first the sound she heard was rain, with the fall wind behind it, rattling the pane of her bedroom window like flung buckshot. She was doing her hair, seated before her dresser mirror with a curling iron which she heated by thrusting it in the chimney of the lamp. She paid the noise no heed until, a moment later, it was repeated. She realized then that it couldn't be rain, that someone must actually be out there tossing up handfuls of pebbles in an effort to attract her attention.

The thought startled her; she laid down the curling iron as she exclaimed, "My land!" Rising, she slipped on a wrapper over her petticoat and crossed the room.

She could see nothing, so she ran the window open. Her room was on the second story of the big house; now, below her and foreshortened from this angle, she made out the figure of a man. Frightened, she would have drawn back and slammed the window shut again if he hadn't called anxiously, "Laurel! It's Wes—Wes Coldbrook!"

It would never do to let him know how her heart leaped, with a quick swelling of something very much like triumph. Instead she rebuked him, in a reproving voice. "Wes! You certainly have your nerve, to stand and throw rocks at my bedroom window. It's as though you thought I were the kind of girl that—"

"Laurel!" His voice, cutting her off, sounded unnatural. "Please! Will you stop talking a minute and listen to me? I'm hurt."

"Hurt!" she gasped.

"Bad! There's a bullet in my shoulder. Will you please let me in?"

She stammered. "I can't do that! Papa isn't here, or the housekeeper. I'm all alone. What would the neighbors—?"

"Damn the neighbors!" Wes Coldbrook exploded. "Can't you understand? I'm in pain! And only you can help me. Now, are you going to come down and open the door for me, or not?"

"Oh all right!" she wailed unhappily.

"The back door," he added sharply as she started to withdraw. "Not the front one. I mustn't be seen!"

Wondering what he could possibly mean, Laurel slammed the window down, thoroughly chilled and trembling. She looked about the room, with its deep four-poster under the ribboned canopy. She caught a glimpse of her reflection in the dresser mirror and she wailed, "I look a *fright!*" Sniffling, she worked at her waist-long blonde hair, twisting it up with a few deft movements of her hands and pinning the pile in place on her neat, small head. A stroke or two of the comb put a few strands in place. A little rice powder on her nose, and a pinch at her cheeks to bring some color into them.

112

Afterward, belting the pale blue wrapper tight around her waist in a manner that she knew would emphasize the swell of her young bosom, she took the oil lamp from the dresser and carried it down through the silent house, the shadows swinging and chasing about her.

When she placed the lamp upon the table and went to pull the hasp on the heavy bolt and open the door, she found Coldbrook leaning there—disheveled, his hat gone, his eyes wild in a face that carried the bruises of his recent battle with Steve Benson. He said hoarsely, "You certainly took your time!" and stepped into the room, and nearly fell on his face.

Laurel caught at his arm to steady him, and saw the blood that soaked the material of his coat; she choked out a gasp of horror, and shrank back with an instinctive dread of touching him. Wes staggered in past her, like a man on his last legs, and now she distinctly smelled the whisky on him. When he gained the table in the middle of the room he managed to let himself into one of the chairs. With his bloodied arm trailing, he placed his other arm on the table and dropped his head upon it, clearly exhausted. Laurel closed the outer door and then stood helplessly watching him, wringing her hands.

His voice muffled by the coatsleeve, Coldbrook said, "Lock the door. And pull the shades. . . ." She moved mechanically to do as he told her, almost without thinking; then returned to the same spot and to the same pointless kneading of her fingers. Finally Wes lifted his head, and it wobbled on his neck. His eyes searched for her.

"You just going to stand there?" he demanded harshly.

She touched a dry tongue to dryer lips. "I—I'll get dressed, and go fetch Dr. Andrews. . . ."

"You will not!" he exclaimed, with such ferocity that she stared, seeing a harshness and a grimness in him that she had never suspected before. He seemed to realize then that he had startled her. "I'm sorry," he muttered. "It's the pain talking. I can't always help what I say . . ."

113

"But—what happened?" she stammered. "Who did this to you?"

"Benson," he told her. "And those friends of his. They're trying to kill me!"

"Steve? Oh, no, Wes! I can't believe it!"

"It's true enough!" He reached with his good hand, trapped her wrist in a grip that hurt. "You always figured he was something on a stick! Well, I tell you he put this bullet in me and now he's set on finishing the job. And all because I dared to show him up, today—him and that woman!"

"There's the sheriff," she suggested.

"No! Not Tom Fawcett!" he cried. "Nor the doctor, either. I tell you, he's turned them all against me. He's got them searching the town. This was the one place I knew they wouldn't have nerve enough to bother me."

The thought struck her: *He came to me!* It filled her with gratification that overcame a little the sight of the blood on his clothing, and the smell of booze. It offset, too, the humiliation of knowing about the woman at the hotel.

There had always been, for Laurel, a conflict in her thoughts of these two men. Steve Benson excited her, as Wes Coldbrook never could, with a sense of maleness and competence; yet, since she was her father's daughter, the thought of marrying Troy Coldbrook's heir was never far from the surface of her mind. It had been a deeply irritating conflict, tugging her constantly in opposite directions. But at that moment she knew suddenly her mind had been made up for her; the conflict was settled.

"I never want to see or hear of Steve Benson again!"

"Good girl!" Wes's voice was thick with pain. He took a long breath, and she saw him wince. "But now we got to do something about that bullet. It's smashed hell out of my shoulder, and it's still in there. It's killing me! And there's no one but you to get it out."

She felt her knees go weak. "I couldn't!"

"You've got to! *Please!*" Suddenly the false toughness ran

114

out of him; his eyes shone with tears and his voice trembled. "Laurel, it hurts. It hurts like the devil!"

"All right." She summoned up her reserves of courage. "I'll—I'll try."

Even thinking of what she was going to have to do put a sick tightness in her throat and she tried to get rid of it by busying herself with collecting the things she supposed she would need. The kitchen was the housekeeper's domain and responsibility, hence it was one room of her home that she seldom entered. She didn't know where anything was kept and had to hunt for the sponge and the cloth for bandages, the hand basin to hold water from the kettle heating on the stove. And a knife—a sharp one! She found a butcher knife in a drawer that looked as though it had a sharp point; she shuddered and had to force herself to pick it up and carry it to the table where Wes Coldbrook sat with hanging head, sodden with pain, no longer able even to offer advice.

There was nothing to do, finally, but get at the job that confronted her.

Wes roused himself enough to help get rid of his jacket, and the shirt that was stuck to him by congealing blood. He had stuffed his pocket handkerchief against the wound in his breast and Laurel had to pull it free. When she did, fresh blood welled out and down his arm, to fall drop by turgid drop from his fingers to the spotless floor. Cheeks bunched tight until her lips were drawn back in a grimace, Laurel used the sponge; the water in the basin quickly turned red. Wes said through clenched teeth, "Bullet must have smashed through the bone and lodged. You should be able to feel it—a lump, back there, under the skin."

She could indeed. She felt her face go suddenly cold and she closed her throat convulsively as icy sweat broke out on her cheeks; but somehow she managed to hold the sickness back. She grasped the handle of the knife with determined firmness.

A quick, slicing jab with the point of the knife, a muffled groan from Wes; something leaped and struck the side of the basin with a faint tinkling sound. The knife slipped from Laurel's hand and she whimpered a little.

Wes drew a shuddering breath. He gasped and said in a voice that sounded unlike his own, "Good girl! But, you got to finish the job. . . ."

With a supreme effort of will she managed to do it, using the lengths of torn cloth to fashion a bulky and awkward bandage. Afterward she worked the pump at the sink and scrubbed her hands furiously, wondering if she would ever get them clean of the feel and the smell of blood. There seemed to be blood everywhere, on the table, the floor, and —a big, frightening stain of it—on the material of her gown. She averted her eyes from all this, thankful that she could leave the mess for the housekeeper or someone else to clean up.

Never knowing how she had managed to keep from fainting, she picked up Wes's coat and put it over his shoulders. "Now," she said. "You need rest. Let me take you in to the couch in the living room."

"No!" he exclaimed, and came surging to his feet, leaning his weight heavily on the table's edge. "I can't stay here. It isn't safe."

She stared. "But, you know they wouldn't dare come for you here. You said, yourself—"

"No place in this town is safe for me," he insisted; he looked haggard and wild. "I've got to get home! My pa will know what to do. Is your father's rig in the shed?" he demanded, as though inspired by a sudden thought.

Laurel nodded. "But you're in no shape even to hitch up the mare. And I don't know how."

"I'll show you," he insisted. "We can do it between us. And you can drive me to the ranch." His hand reached and closed upon her arm; his eyes held a feverish shine. "Do this for me, Laurel," he said huskily, "and I swear that anything you want—anything I can do for you—"

Looking up at him, she felt a hard core of satisfaction form and settle inside her. Being her father's daughter, she

116

knew an advantage when she saw one. And in that moment she knew that, after tonight, Wes Coldbrook was hers and so was Keystone—everything that a young woman of spoiled needs could possibly ask for. They were all hers because she had earned them; and if, for just an instant, the thought of Steve Benson still rose to trouble her, she put it resolutely aside and locked her heart against it. In the long run, this was really what she wanted.

After all, Steve Benson had shown his true colors. If he preferred that woman at the hotel, then he could have her!

"All right, Wes honey," she said soothingly—taking charge, as her instinct told her Wes Coldbrook's woman would always need to take charge. "Just give me a minute to get some clothes on—and find something warm of Papa's for you, so we can get rid of those awful bloodstained rags. Then we'll hitch up the mare and be out of this town.

"Just stop trembling. You're going to be all right. . . ."

Strangely, all her own terror was forgotten and replaced by a calm that seemed incapable of ruffling. She had never before hitched the bay mare to the rig, that was kept in the shed behind her father's house, but with Wes giving instructions she managed to get the straps and the buckles right, though her cold hands fumbled awkwardly at the job. Then, seated beside Wes on the buggy's seat, with a heavy laprobe spread across their knees for warmth, she sent the mare out into the windy night and turned the rig downhill toward Main.

The town looked no different, and yet it seemed to Laurel there was an odd air of danger. She told herself it was only imagination. Main Street was nearly deserted, though once she saw a group of men moving through the shadows along one side of the street, with the grim and silent purposefulness of a search party. She glanced at Wes; his face, in a vagrant gleam of lamplight from a window they passed, looked pale and scared. His hand clutched the buggy's ironwork, in a way that suggested he might leap out and run at any moment. "One more block to go," she told him quietly.

Just at the end of the street where the last houses fell away and the road to Keystone stretched away through the sage, they saw the bobbing lantern put its small, swinging spark against the blackness. Laurel heard Wes' gasp of alarm. Too late now to turn the buggy; her hands tightened on the leathers. "Get down!" she ordered. "Quick—down out of sight. . . ." He obeyed without question. She felt him twisting and turning as he slid off the seat, heard him groan once. Then he was huddled on the buggy's floor, pressing against her legs, and she hurriedly smoothed the robe in such a way that it hid and covered him.

She was barely in time. As she settled herself and took the reins again, the guard came walking across the dust with a circle of lantern light swaying about his legs and glinting from the barrel of a rifle he carried under one arm. He came to a halt, lifting his lantern by its bale; its glow invaded the shadows below the buggy's top and Laurel squinted against it, frowning as she tried to avert her eyes. "Please," she exclaimed. "Whatever in the world—?"

"Oh—Miss Whitney!" Quickly he lowered the light from her face. The man was Ollie Spangler, who ran the dry goods store. The incongruous sight of him with a gun under his arm, halting traffic on a blustery autumn night, was in itself startling enough. It helped make her puzzled reaction sound convincing.

"Whatever is going on, Mr. Spangler?"

"You ain't heard? A bad business, Miss Whitney. Whole town's worked up. It's Wes Coldbrook—he's supposed to be hiding somewhere, hurt. And we got orders from the sheriff to stop him leaving if we can."

"But what could the sheriff want with Wes?"

Spangler told her, "Abel Gannon died tonight. Before he did, he said young Coldbrook was the man slugged him with a gunbarrel and crushed his skull. The sheriff calls it murder."

"I don't believe it!" The words were driven from her.

"Afraid it's true, all right. Earlier—before Gannon died

118

—there was some shooting. That's how the boy got a bullet in him."

Laurel Whitney felt suddenly faint. Her hands, shaking with the cold and with nerves, could scarcely hold the lines.

"Anyway," the man with the lantern said, "that's why I stopped you. I got orders to take a look at any wagon traffic rolling out of town, this time of night. Sheriff thinks he might try to make a sneak. Hope you'll excuse me."

"Oh, that's all right. I—" She fought the shallowness of her breathing. "I'm just taking a little ride out to the Penhallow place. Dimity Penhallow's been after me to drop out and spend the night with her sometime, and—and I just thought, on the spur of the moment—"

"Yes, ma'am. Well—have a nice ride." He stepped back, lifting the lantern in salute. Laurel nodded and slapped the reins against the mare's rump. The buggy jolted forward over the hard ruts, and in a matter of minutes the last lights of the town fell back and the night surrounded her.

There was a stirring at her feet; Wes's voice reached her, muffled and barely distinct. "Are we in the clear?"

Her lips felt wooden. "I think so. But maybe you'd better stay where you are till we're sure."

Silence. Then, his voice again:

"Laurel, you're a brick! I—I'm just glad you didn't believe any of that stuff he told you. I'm glad you could see it's all lies—something that bastard Steve Benson has put into people's heads!" Laurel rode on, her hands stiff on the reins, her eyes straight ahead. She knew he was waiting for an answer; when he got none his voice came clearer, touched with alarm: "You *do* know it's a lie?"

Laurel's mouth settled more firmly. "I'll take you to your pa," she said in a steady voice. "He'll know what to do." A moment later she added, "And the marriage. We'll want to arrange it right away. . . ."

XVI

It was in the sheriff's office that Steve Benson first learned he had been named Abel Gannon's heir. That he was now the owner of Gannon's ranch, and without having need to use the loan from the Denver bank, hardly registered at all; he was too deeply shocked by the news of Gannon's death, and by the report—confirming his half-formed guess —that Gannon's last words had put the blame squarely onto Wes Coldbrook and Burke Sully. He stared at Doc Andrews, who had brought the news. He made the old doctor repeat again what the dying man had said. And then he turned a grim look on Sheriff Tom Fawcett, and the other manhunters jamming the clapboard office.

"Now there's no two ways about it," he said. "We got to find Coldbrook!"

The sheriff stroked his silky black brush of mustache, his expression deeply troubled. It was a bad spot for Tom Fawcett. A sincere and conscientious officer, it was still natural that he would be reluctant to lock horns with a powerful man like Troy Coldbrook—one, moreover, that he'd known and respected. Yesterday's clash at Horseshoe Meadow had been possible to pass off as a misunderstanding; but this was different. This was a charge against Coldbrook's only son. It wasn't in the cards that Troy Coldbrook would soon forgive the man—lawman or otherwise—that brought his boy in to hang.

Joe Niles said bleakly, "Nobody's getting anywhere very fast. We've found his bronc where he left it in the alley, behind the doc's, but no sign of Wes. Either he's lying doggo somewhere we ain't thought of looking, or he's managed to give us the slip."

"It doesn't seem possible," someone else commented. "Not the way we've been going through this town!"

"Well, there's something we've missed," Benson insisted.

120

"We know he's hurt—probably bad hurt—so he couldn't have got far. Then, what are we doing wrong? Why haven't we found him?"

Niles said, "Looks like we better start from scratch again. Either that, or take an army out to Keystone and see if somehow or other he made it there."

"I'd hate to do it that way," Tom Fawcett said bleakly, "if there's any other choice. Before I go to Keystone, with or without an army, I want some good reason to think he's there. Because I'm afraid Troy would make a showdown fight of it, before he'd give the boy up. . . ."

It was then they got the first sure clue, when Dan Whitney and Ollie Spangler came rushing in together. The banker's face was gray as putty, and his hands shook; he babbled almost hysterically as he told what he had found on returning home, moments before—blood spattered on the kitchen table and floor; a basin of bloody water, a flattened bullet, torn bandages; a bloodsoaked coat and shirt that could only be Wes Coldbrook's. The sheriff and Steve Benson exchanged a long look. "Of course!" Benson exclaimed. "He went to Laurel! We should have thought of that."

"But she's vanished!" Dan Whitney exclaimed. "That—that monster's took her away with him, after forcing her to dig the bullet out of him! My Laurel—being put through an ordeal like that!" In his shock, he no longer remembered that Wes Coldbrook had always been his favorite candidate for his daughter's hand.

Ollie Spangler spoke up then, to tell about passing Laurel Whitney through on the north road out of town. "I never thought nothing about it," the man insisted. "I remember saying it seemed kind of late, but she told me something about riding out to spend the night at the Penhallows'. I guess I should have looked closer, to see if there was anyone else in that buggy with her. It just didn't occur to me."

Benson suggested, "Maybe we're guessing wrong. Maybe she did go to Penhallow's." But he knew, in the light of everything else, that it was a vain thought.

121

"No—no," her father said, shaking his head and passing a fleshy hand across his cheeks. "We can check, but I know we'll find she's never been there. She must be somewhere with that murderer!"

"They're at Keystone," Joe Niles said bluntly. "Wes is in bad trouble, and he only knows to run to his pa for help." He looked at the sheriff. "Looks like it calls for that army we spoke about. We'll ride out there and tear the place down if we have to."

Fawcett considered, scowling. "No," he said heavily. "You just don't do that to Troy Coldbrook. He deserves more respect—and a chance to show he knows his duty to the law. . . . I'll go. I'll ask him point blank to turn the boy over. Doc, Wes will probably be needing you, if he's as bad hurt as we're led to think."

Seth Andrews nodded, and Steve Benson said, "I'm going too. I'm the one that shot Wes," he pointed out. "I won't have Troy thinking I was afraid to face him. If he has anything to say to me, I want to hear and answer it."

"You don't go without me," Joe Niles told his partner sharply. "That's final!"

Tom Fawcett made his decision. "All right," the sheriff said, nodding to Benson. "That ought to be enough to do the job. You, and Joe Niles, and the doc and me. It's enough to show we won't be bluffed, that we mean business—but not enough, I hope, to put Troy on the prod. We'll give him his chance, and see what he wants to do about it. . . ."

Keystone headquarters seemed quiet enough, tonight—strangely quiet. Lights showed in the main house and the quarters of the crew, yet things were so still that a rattling of dry leaves on the branches of the poplar trees around the house came distinctly on the night wind.

The sheriff had halted his party at the very edge of the yard; here, the wagon road turned in beneath the tall skeleton scaffolding of a peeled-pole gateway, that held an oil lantern burning high on its uprights. They made a tight

122

group surrounding Doc Andrews' rig and listened to the stillness, and to the stomping of their own horses. Joe Niles said, "Somehow I don't much like this. It don't seem right. Where is everybody?"

Steve Benson answered him. "They're waiting for us. Why do you think that lantern is up there?" He indicated it, swaying on the gatepost, clearly pointing them out to the eyes of anyone watching from the spread of buildings ahead of them.

"I can take care of that quick enough!" Niles stirred in the saddle and the gun slid from his holster. Tom Fawcett stopped him before he could take a shot at the lantern and blow it off its nail.

"No! That's just asking for a fight. Leave the thing burn," he went on, "we'll make it work for us. Niles, you and Seth stay here while Steve and I ride in. I can't really believe Troy Coldbrook would set a trap; but if that's what it is, they won't dare spring it if they see we're leaving witnesses behind. They'll have to walk easy."

"That makes sense," Benson agreed, though Joe Niles grumbled a little. While Niles and the doctor waited under the gateway, the other two rode forward, with nothing about their manner to suggest the high mounting of tension inside them as they took the slight climb toward the high ground where the big house stood.

The biting tang of chimney smoke came to them, carried on the downdraft sweeping along the rise. The house had a square of lawn, that was littered with leaves whipping in an occasional golden streak past the lighted windows. As they pulled up, Burke Sully's familiar voice sang out: "That's far enough!" A moment later the Keystone foreman came walking out of the shadows under the veranda roof, and down the steps to a wide-placed stand in the path, facing them. "You don't need to bother getting out of your saddles."

"Do you know who you're talking to?" Tom Fawcett demanded. The light was poor, but there was enough leakage from the windows of the house to show faces, palely, and the general outline of a man's shape. "Burke, this is the sheriff!"

"Hell, I know it's the sheriff," Sully retorted. "It means nothing to me—we got no business."

"No one said we did. I'm looking for Wes Coldbrook."

"He ain't here. Ain't been all evening."

"Oh? What about Troy? And Ada?"

"Them, neither!" the foreman snapped. "They took off somewheres. When they come back I'll tell them you was asking for them. But, right now, like I said, there's no point you even getting out of the saddle."

While Tom Fawcett stared at the man, through the chill darkness, Steve Benson put in a word. "Lots of light burning in the house," he pointed out mildly. "I could have sworn I just saw someone move past one of the windows in the living room. Looked a lot like Troy."

"Who's calling me a liar?" Burke Sully demanded; his head thrust forward as he tried to make out the sheriff's companion.

Someone cried, "It's Benson!" The voice was Vic Gilmore's. He was standing near a corner of the house, below the veranda railing. A vagrant track of light glimmered off the metal of a gun in his hand. "Let me take him, Sully! I ain't paid the sonofabitch back yet for using his fist on me yesterday, in town!"

"Forget it!" Burke Sully retorted, and a quick tightening in Benson eased a trifle as Gilmore let the gun lower from its direct point on his chest. Meanwhile the ranchyard seemed suddenly to be filled with men. They came drifting up—from the direction of the barn, the bunkshack, every point in the perimeter of the ranch buildings. They should have been proof enough that this visit had not been unexpected, or taken anyone by surprise.

"Well, sheriff?" the foreman prodded. "It's too cold to stand out here arguing."

"I agree," Tom Fawcett said calmly. "So I think we'll just come inside and wait for Troy. . . ."

He actually started to swing a leg over the cantle of his saddle, as though to dismount. That brought a roar from Burke Sully. "Damn it, no! I said—"

And then, abruptly, the big door swung open, letting a broad path of light fall across the porch. Through this path Troy Coldbrook himself came striding to the very edge of the steps. There, hatless and in his shirtsleeves, he placed his fists on his hips and he spoke in angry impatience. "Oh, hell, Tom!" he told the sheriff. "Do you have to have it spelled out for you? I gave Burke orders that I wouldn't see you—I got too many other things on my mind to bother with you tonight. Now, are you satisfied that you've made me say it to your face?"

The sheriff settled back into the leather. He looked across the little distance at the angry cattleman. He said quietly, "Don't worry about sparing my feelings—you never have, before. I'll ask you just once, Troy. And from you I expect a straight answer.

"Is Wes here, or isn't he?"

For a long moment Troy Coldbrook was silent. He glared through the tangled thicket of his brows and said, at last, "All right, Tom—if you insist on making this a showdown. I was hoping to avoid one . . . Yes, the boy is here—nearly out of his head with pain, but talking clear enough that I got a pretty good idea what you, and that bastard with you, are doing here at Keystone."

"And what is that?" the sheriff demanded.

"Come off it! Benson tried to murder him; failing that he's sold you on taking the boy in on some trumped-up charge that I don't even want to know about!"

Steve Benson said, "Troy, he's lying to you!"

Coldbrook wheeled on him, his voice shaking suddenly with rage. "You devil! You dare to call my boy a liar? I admit you had me fooled, Benson. I thought you was just another worthless greasy-sacker; but I can see now, you're somebody a damn sight craftier than I ever figured! All this past year—all the time I was letting myself be hustled around that stinkin' Europe—you must have been working night and day, trying to undercut me and drag the Cold-brooks down. First you weasel your way in with Abel Gannon and nearly grab that range of his out from under my nose. Then you bring that woman and her bastard here, to try and blacken the very name of Coldbrook. And now—this!

"Well, I've had enough! For once, you've gone too far—even if you have got the law to do your dirty work. . . ."

"Now hold on!" Tom Fawcett tried to break in. Coldbrook silenced him.

"I'm talking to Benson! And I'm laying it on the table: If you want a fight, mister, then you can have it. And it'll be the sorriest day you ever seen the sun come up. Because, you ain't big enough to stand to me. I'll smash you so flat that—"

"Don't go for a gun, Benson!"

It was Vic Gilmore who shouted; Steve Benson was never to know whether the puncher really thought he saw him start a move toward his holster. There was only a startled second, while the warning registered. Then, before he had time to make any move at all, the Keystone man's gun-muzzle streaked flame.

He felt the tap of concussion against his cheek—the bullet missed him that narrowly, as in belated reflex he spilled sidewards in the saddle. He heard Tom Fawcett's angry shout. He was pawing at his unbuttoned windbreaker, and the holster that lay against his leg, when he glimpsed Vic Gilmore lowering his gunbarrel after the recoil, lining for a second shot.

XVII

THEN ANOTHER gun spoke and its report overlaid the echoes of the first. The mingled sounds of the two weapons bounced flatly from the dark wall of the house. Vic Gilmore, hit, spun violently across a square of spilled window-light and went down onto his knees, dropping his revolver. Benson's horse, shying, stepped around uneasily and he dragged the rein to settle him, while he fumbled his own sixshooter out of the holster.

Tom Fawcett, with a smoking gun in his hand, let his warning carry above the confusion in the yard. "Let's have no more of that!" he cried furiously. "Troy, I hold you responsible if this bunch gets out of hand. I advise you to hold a close rein on them!"

"Nobody tells me how to manage my crew!" Coldbrook snapped, and turning to his foreman, said, "Burke—take a look at him."

The man the sheriff had shot was still on his knees, a hand pressed against his ribs, and swearing furiously. Burke Sully, without any more than glancing in his direction, said curtly, "Don't sound to me like he's much damaged. . . ."

There was a noise of hoofs and spinning wheels. Steve Benson turned quickly in the saddle as Joe Niles and Doc Andrews came up the road from the gate, driving their horses hard. Niles had pulled out ahead of the doctor's rig, and was shouting questions as he drew rein beside his partner with his bronc's shoes scattering gritty dust. "Who's shooting?" he demanded belligerently.

"Take it easy," snapped Benson.

It seemed to him the situation was still dangerously close to a general explosion. Sheriff Fawcett appeared to share his thought. "Troy," the officer said tightly, "I don't figure you're willing to let anyone tell you anything!"

"I want nothing from you!" Coldbrook answered flatly. "Not when you take sides with my enemies!"

"That ain't so!" But Tom Fawcett might as well have been shouting at a brick wall.

Now Seth Andrews was pulling his team around in a wide half circle and hauling in on the leathers. The horses moved restlessly as the ground wind whipped away the dust and settled it; and Doc, who had heard the last of Coldbrook's words, called out to him, "You've known me longer than any man here, Troy. How about it? Will you listen to me? Or do you just figure any man is a liar and a skunk when he dares to tell you anything you don't like to hear?"

Coldbrook glared at his old friend, shoulders hunched and face craggy in the wash of light from the open door. "I'll listen," he said at last, grudgingly. "But I don't promise to believe a damn word!"

"You'll believe it," Andrews replied, "if you know what's good for you! Troy, your son's a murderer! Abel Gannon died tonight, naming him the man who bent a gunbarrel across his skull. If that ain't bad enough, Wes sneaked into my house earlier in the evening and tried to finish Gannon off, and shut his mouth for good. It took a bullet from Steve Benson's gun to stop him.

"Now, go on and call me a liar if you want to, Troy; but deep down I think you know I've never told you nothing but the truth!"

Steve Benson almost had it in him to feel sorry for Troy Coldbrook, in that moment. Stubborn and headstrong as he was, the rancher had no ready answer to what Seth Andrews had laid out for him. His mouth opened and closed; he lifted a finger to point it at the doctor, then slowly let his arm fall again.

It was the sheriff who broke the silence. "If the lad is innocent, Troy, he'll be man enough to face his accusers. Let us in so we can talk to him. Can't you see, it's the only way to settle this?"

"All you want to do is arrest him and drag him off to that jail of yours!" Coldbrook exclaimed bitterly. "And he's in no shape."

"I'll be the best judge of that, Troy," the doctor pointed out patiently. "If he's hurt, it's my job to help him—and I want to. So, quit acting like a fool and let us in. You know, in the end, you got no choice. You can't make things any way but worse, by keeping on like this."

Troy Coldbrook seemed to struggle with himself, as though

128

listening to inward, brawling voices. His thick chest swelled then on a drawn breath, and he said harshly, "All right, damn you! Come on in. But you'll leave your guns outside."

"Now, just a minute!" Tom Fawcett cried. "You can't order the law around!"

"Give him his way, Tom," Steve Benson said quietly. "He's trying to make a concession. Here's my gun." He flung back the tails of his windbreaker, unhooked his holster belt and handed it across to Joe Niles. "Hold it for me till we come out."

His partner appeared darkly skeptical, but he took the belt and slung it across his saddle horn; Benson dismounted and dropped the reins to ground-anchor them. As he did, tension seemed to tighten in the ranks of the watching crew. The sheriff glanced about, still not moving, still reluctant; but Doc Andrews seemed satisfied.

"I never wear a gun," the old man pointed out. "Always figured they're a lot of damned nonsense, that accomplish nothing but to keep someone like me in too much business!" Wrapping the reins to the grabiron of his seat he climbed painfully down, a real effort. "Bring that fellow over in the light," he ordered then, nodding to a pair of the ranch crew who had got Vic Gilmore back onto his feet. "Let me take a look. . . ."

By the glow from a window Andrews made a quick examination of the puncher's bulletscored ribs. "No real damage," he pronounced, straightening with a grunt. "Bullet only sliced his bacon a little. Take him to the bunkhouse and clean him up, and I'll see him again when more important things are settled." As they led Gilmore away, he laid his scowl on the sheriff. "Looks like we're waiting on you, Tom."

Fawcett swore under his breath, but passed his gun over to Joe Niles. Through a wordless stillness they moved toward the house steps, fallen leaves crunching beneath their boots. Troy Coldbrook watched them come, and at the last moment swung aside and motioned them to precede him through the door.

They were in a huge living room that stretched straight across the whole front of the house. Looking at the massive furnishings—the rawhide chairs, the solid tables and massive ceiling beams and deep fieldstone fireplace with the rack of antlers above it, the stand of rifles and shotguns against one wall—one would hardly suspect that a woman had ever lived here. In thirty years, Ada Coldbrook had made no impression on this house at all.

Now she stood, like a gray ghost, and stared in apprehension as these men tramped inside; her eyes searched each face in turn. Steve Benson's gaze moved on to the person who stood across the room with her back against the rough plastered wall as though for support. His eyes met Laurel Whitney's and for a moment they shared a look that neither was ever likely to forget.

Benson was shouldered roughly aside, then, and Troy Coldbrook strode past him to the fireplace where a burning pine log put out heat enough to nullify the chill blast let in by the still-open door. In a chair that had been pulled up close to the crackling fire, Wes Coldbrook sprawled with his head thrown back and his eyes closed.

The men trooped over to him and stood silently eyeing him a moment. He looked to be asleep, knocked out by pain and the exhausting of his reserves of strength. His face was graved by deep lines of suffering and his skin was as colorless as the bandages that covered his injury.

Ungently, Troy Coldbrook bent and seized his son by the unhurt arm and gave it a peremptory shaking. Wes groaned a little, at first without stirring. Then his waxen lids stirred and lifted; his head rolled a little on his neck as his eyes sought focus. "What—?" he mumbled. Suddenly he seemed to register the faces looking down at him. Fear and alarm drained his face of whatever color was left in it, and he straightened convulsively in the chair.

Coldbrook gave it to him straight, and bluntly. "Son,

130

Gannon's dead. And these men claim you're the one that done for him. What have you got to say?"

Wes looked from one face to another, his mouth working and panic brimming in his eyes. But no words came and his father's jaw set hard. "We're waiting. . . ."

"It ain't true!" Wes blurted, the words spilling from him. "It wasn't me, Pa. It—it was Burke! Yeah! Gannon must have been all mixed up. The three of us were there, and Burke got tough with him. Pa, I told him not to! I tried to stop him—"

"Why, you sonofabitch!" Burke Sully stood in the doorway, having followed the others inside. His face congested with dark fury, he yelled at Wes: "I told you never to try to lay that on me!" Too late, they saw the gun held naked in his hand. There was a single piercing shriek from Laurel Whitney. The gun spoke, loosing flame and sound and a writhing ring of muzzle smoke. The bullet struck Wes solidly, drove him flopping back into the depths of the big chair and pinned him there.

Quite deliberately, Troy Coldbrook drew his long-barreled Colt revolver. While Steve Benson stood frozen in horror, hardly even remembering that his own gun and belt were hanging on the pommel of Joe Niles' saddle, the rancher took aim and fired. The two shots mingled. A look of astonishment crossed Sully's face, and then it was wiped away by vacuous nothingness. His jaw fell open, his eyes rolled into his head; after that he was going down, with his shoulders sliding across the plaster and wood at the door's edge, and the still-smoking gun dropped from his lifeless hand and hit the floor before his body did.

Troy Coldbrook looked at the man he had killed, and his face was iron. He lifted his eyes to the sheriff then and told him, "Make what you like of this—and be damned to you. But I said once, in this house I'm the law. I lay it down, and I enforce it!"

Fawcett breathed deeply and shook his head. "I ain't

saying a word, Troy. Could be you've saved the county the expense of a hanging. That is, if—"

He couldn't finish it. Instead he looked toward Doc Andrews who was already bending over the body of Wes Coldbrook, sprawled half out of the big chair by the fireplace. Andrews met his eyes, and shook his head in confirmation. "The boy's dead. . . ."

Steve Benson saw Ada Coldbrook's tragic, stricken face, and had to look away from it. At the same moment, there came the trampling of boots and shouting of voices outside, as the ranch crew converged on the open door in the wake of the shooting.

Troy Coldbrook said harshly, "Damn it, keep that mob out of here!" and was himself the first one to reach the door, stepping past his dead foreman's crumpled shape. "Get away!" he bawled. "If I need you here, I'll call you." He swung the door shut in the faces of his own crew, but not quite in time to stop Joe Niles. The latter caught the heavy panel on his shoulder and shoved through, letting it slam to behind him and, with gun leveled, he peered around a little wildly, searching for danger to his partner.

Steve Benson said, "You can put it away, Joe. Everything's settled."

Niles seemed to take in the situation, then. He looked at the dead foreman, and at Ada Coldbrook on her knees beside her son's body with her face in her hands. He looked stunned, but he slid the gun into its holster. "My God!" he exclaimed, in a shocked voice.

To Coldbrook, Benson said, "Troy, I'm sorry. I never thought for it to end like this!" The rancher looked at him as though without even seeing him. Moving woodenly, Troy Coldbrook turned away and crossed the room to stand looking at the face of his son. After a moment he leaned and got his arms under the dead boy and lifted him. He straightened, settling his burden, and turned again and moved through the room's stillness toward the stairs that rose to the second floor. At the foot of them he paused, swinging about to look for Steve Benson.

He said, in a heavy voice, "I'll ask you to do something for me."

"Of course," Benson waited, puzzled.

"I want my grandson. Looks like I made a poor job of it, with his pa. Looks like I expected too much—and demanded too little. His mother always secretly believed I brought him up wrong, and I guess this proves it—shows maybe I ought to have let Ada have more say in his raising.

"Well, maybe I get a second chance. Maybe I don't deserve one; but I'd like to try and make up for the way I failed, the first time. So, will you fetch the youngun here?"

"Tomorrow," Benson said. "First thing. And glad to do it."

Troy nodded. He looked as though there was something more he wanted to say, but appeared to change his mind. He turned and tramped slowly up the stairs, poker-straight, with the dead weight of his son in his arms.

Doc Andrews murmured something to the dead boy's mother, helped her to her feet. In a continuing silence, the others watched him go with her across the room and up the steps, in the wake of Troy Coldbrook. Tom Fawcett broke the silence, finally. He cleared his throat, pawing at his heavy mustache with one hand, and indicated the stiffening body of Burke Sully. "Better get that damn thing out of here!" he muttered. "I'll fetch a couple of the boys." He strode out of the house, as though happy to escape the room, and its pungent sting of powdersmoke.

With Joe Niles watching him narrowly, Steve Benson turned to Laurel Whitney who had not once moved from the spot where she had stood and watched the unfolding of the last act of this tragedy.

"You should be getting home," he said. "I left your pa worried sick about you. I'll take you into town."

She came to him and stood close, looking pale and disheveled, a frown between her brows. She touched her tongue

133

to dry lips. "The baby," she said faintly. "It really was his?"

Benson nodded. "Yes."

"And—all the things I thought about you, and said— Oh, Steven! I've been such an awful fool!"

His shoulders lifted on a long breath. He shook his head. "It doesn't matter."

"No. I can see it doesn't. It really doesn't matter at all, does it?" she exclaimed. She lifted a hand to place it on his sleeve, but let it fall again without touching him. "You loved me," she said in a heavy voice. "And I've killed it."

He chose his words carefully. "Maybe it never really was there, Laurel. You and me—I got a feeling we'd never have made a pair."

"And now, you've found someone that will?"

The picture of Ruth Faris, dominating every other thought, made him nod. "That's my feeling. I aim to find out if she feels the same—first chance I get to ask her."

"I see." The blue doll's eyes studied his face. Laurel nodded finally and said, with more maturity in her voice then he remembered ever hearing there before, "Good luck, Steven. You deserve it all." She turned away, took her cloak from a chair where she had laid it. "I'm ready to go home, now."

Steve Benson silently helped her on with the cloak. He took her arm then and, still without speaking, opened the door for her. She averted her eyes from the body of Burke Sully as they walked past, out of that house, into the clean autumn night.